"May I help you?" Claire blurted out.

Round dark eyes in a long face glimmered with interest. One or two loose strands of silver highlighted his hairline at the temples. She stared in surprise.

He dusted himself off, then shot her another look laced with curiosity. "Can I help *you*?" His voice had a deep Southern drawl that made him sound like a sheriff. Something about him was familiar, although she was sure she wouldn't have forgotten him if she'd met him before.

"Well…this is my house," Claire explained, feeling her cheeks warm and wondering why she was blushing.

The man studied her as if she were making it up. "You're the owner?" he mused in a tone mingled with doubt. "Are you the one selling the house?"

Claire gave her head a small shake. "I was, but I changed my mind and decided to move in."

The stranger's jaw softened, and it made him look crestfallen over the news. "You're not selling." The man's face clouded. "But I thought—"

"No." She bit her lip, oddly disheartened to be disappointing him. She wasn't sure why…

Danielle Thorne is a Southern girl who treasures home and family. Besides books, she loves travel, history, cookies and naps. She's eternally thankful for the women she calls friends. Danielle is the author of over a dozen novels with elements of romance, adventure and faith. You'll often find her in the mountains or at the beach. She currently lives south of Atlanta with her sweetheart of thirty years and two cats.

Books by Danielle Thorne

Love Inspired

His Daughter's Prayer
A Promise for His Daughter

Visit the Author Profile page at LoveInspired.com.

A Promise for His Daughter

Danielle Thorne

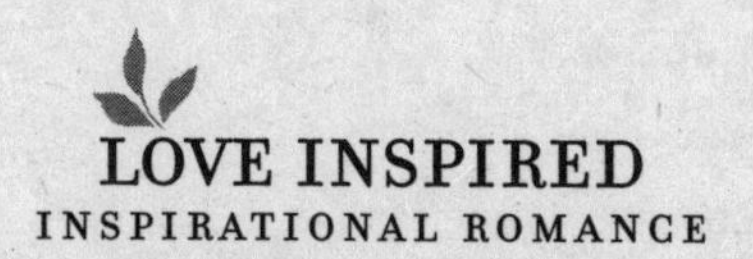

LOVE INSPIRED®
INSPIRATIONAL ROMANCE

Recycling programs for this product may not exist in your area.

ISBN-13: 978-1-335-75926-9

A Promise for His Daughter

For questions and comments about the quality of this book, please contact us at CustomerService@Harlequin.com.

Love Inspired
22 Adelaide St. West, 41st Floor
Toronto, Ontario M5H 4E3, Canada
www.LoveInspired.com

Printed in U.S.A.

Yet setteth he the poor on high from affliction,
and maketh him families like a flock.
—*Psalm* 107:41

To my mother, who knew no family
yet sacrificed everything to have her own.

Chapter One

The rickety roof of a covered bridge emerged out of the morning mist as the Georgia highway narrowed. Claire Woodbury slowed the compact car before the blacktop gave way to the clackety wood planks under the vaulted tin roof. "We made it," she cheered to Emily. But there was no response. Claire glanced up into the rearview mirror and saw the precious two-year-old had slipped off into dreamland in time for the arrival to her new home.

Henny House. No more apartments. No more court visits. The quaint town of Kudzu Creek would be the fresh start they both needed even if Miss Henny was no longer with them. A tender lump made her throat ache. She could hardly believe Miss Henny had willed her the family home. It would make caring for Emily easier, and the small town of Kudzu Creek would be a wonderful place to bring up a child.

Sunshine pierced lingering tendrils of fog and lit the ivy-tangled roadside. The peaceful picture it made boosted Claire's faith. Leaving Birmingham after so many years had been tough, but Kudzu Creek was as close to a home as she'd ever known even if she'd only lived there a few years. Miss Henny had been the best foster mom in the world, and Claire wanted something like that for Emily. Since Emily's mother, Dori, had died, Claire was all the little girl had. It'd been easy to promise her best friend she would raise her little girl right.

Claire opened a window. The morning breeze mingled with wildflowers and flooded the car. She glanced back to watch Emily's snow-white locks flutter around her precious face. She looked like the angel her mother had been.

A Welcome sign emerged from the hazy early morning summer humidity and announced they'd officially reached the town limits of Kudzu Creek. A smile curved Claire's cheek. Not far from where Dori grew up, and just an hour's drive to the Florida panhandle, Kudzu Creek's outskirts were as lush as Claire remembered.

A few sprawling houses, straggling pines and moss-dripping oaks lined the highway into town like Georgian sentinels. Soon, the homes became more modest and sidewalks and iron streetlamps took over. A converted shotgun-style house was now a dentist's office, and just past its blue sign, the street became cobblestoned with well-preserved brick buildings on either side. Passing Miss Henny's church, Claire watched for the town center where a flagged mast stood at attention with bushy pink azaleas at its feet.

The car trundled around the flagpole and past the coffee shop. It'd been reestablished as a kitschy-looking diner called Southern Fried Kudzu. "Interesting," Claire murmured. She spotted a gift shop she'd looked up online then reached Maple Grove Lane and made the familiar left-hand turn onto Miss Henny's street.

The older homes on Maple Grove Lane were a mix of styles that evidenced the slow growth of the town through the centuries. Most had immaculate yards with enormous maple trees and gardens along the sidewalks. Claire's pulse danced as she neared her old address. Like her foster mom, the eccentric Henny House was a mishmash of opinions that did not fit in with the rest of the neighborhood. The old Victorian house had a low roofline that hovered over two asymmetrical gables. Stunted roman columns perched along the rail of a long white porch. At the far end, a gazebo looked like it'd been shipped in from a Gatsby movie set. Architecturally, the structure was a hot mess but, charming and unique, it was Miss Henny in a nutshell and that was what had brought Claire back.

She narrowed her eyes as she slowed the car along the sidewalk in front of the house. Paint was peeling everywhere, and the porch leaned oddly to the left. The roof looked sunken in. Claire's floating heart suddenly dropped like a stone. A few repairs she'd expected, but not this much damage. A black-and-white For Sale sign was planted in the front yard beside a fire ant mound. Why hadn't the real estate company removed the sign after she'd informed them she'd changed her mind?

She looked down the street toward Ms. Olivia's red-brick house. Miss Henny's quite elderly and well-informed neighbor always had the answers to what was happening on Maple Grove Lane. She'd bet Ms. Olivia would know.

With a sinking feeling, Claire eyeballed the noxious ivy that had grown around the porch columns and up to the gutter. One end of the rusting drain pipe was drooping like it'd given up. She swallowed down a ripple of panic. The place was in worse condition than she'd thought. She knew Miss Henny had intended to do updates, but she'd grown old too fast after her foster daughter had left for college. It was up to Claire to follow through now that Miss Henny had passed on. The unconventional house had real potential and room to build the pottery studio she'd always dreamed of. Running a ceramist business was her plan to bring in income to care for Emily. She braced herself. With a lot of hard work and imagination, it could be the gem of Kudzu Creek. Miss Henny had left some money, but time had caught up with the house, too, and that meant dollar signs.

Claire made a mental note to remind the real estate agent she'd decided not to sell. Climbing out to stretch, she estimated how much the work needing to be done outside would eat into her budget. She stared at the forlorn two-story and tried to imagine it with gleaming windows, an onyx door and a fresh coat of eggplant-purple paint. She pictured a bronze plaque beside the door: *Artist in Residence.*

Gathering her courage, Claire reached into the back of the car for Emily, who folded easily over her shoulder without stirring. They'd left before daylight and the little toddler had been chatty and giggly the entire trip. Claire knew Emily didn't understand the momentous occasion, but soon her best friend's daughter would have her own space and all the things Claire had never had moving from one foster home to the next. *If* she could salvage this house and start a successful at-home business with her pottery studio.

She juggled her purse with the toddler while she climbed the cracked cement driveway. Moss was creeping over the edges of the slight incline. Some of the steps to the front door were rotting in various places. Claire eyed the length of the porch in dismay as she fumbled for her keys. She inserted the house key into the tarnished handle of the faded front door. It pushed ajar before she turned the lock.

Her heart fluttered in surprise. The key box that allowed real estate agents to show the house was gone. Claire opened the door the rest of the way with her shoulder, and it groaned on its hinges. The last person inside must have forgotten to lock it, she decided, unless they were still here. They were probably going to remove the sign today.

She looked around. The foyer was empty, and its wooden floors smelled musty. The uncarpeted staircase crept up to the second floor. In the stillness, she tried to imagine she could hear Miss Henny in the kitchen listening to her favorite radio talk show, but Miss Henny, like Dori, was gone and it seemed she'd taken the soul of the house with her.

A bang echoed from somewhere in the back. "Hello?" she called.

"Hello," called a friendly voice. "Back here."

Claire slipped into the parlor and laid Emily down on one of the sheet-covered sofas.

She glanced across the foyer to the empty study then walked down the hall as something rattled again from the kitchen.

Claire peered around the doorframe with curiosity. The eighties-era cabinets were still there. So were the green-laminate countertops that had once been stylish.

A large bay window over the breakfast nook was fogged and several panes needed replacement. Faded ivy wallpaper border curled above it like ribbon. Beside the table, a pair of dark khakis stretched up to the ceiling.

Claire froze. The tapered legs were planted on a stepladder that belonged in the pantry. A blue chambray shirttail draped over the top of the slacks. “Hello?” Claire realized she’d spoken in almost a whimper and took a deep breath. Before she could repeat herself, a hammer struck a ceiling tile with a bang.

Showers of white crumbs rained over the intruder and down to the floor. A head of short hair trimmed along a sunburned neckline cocked back toward the ceiling, and so did the hammer, ready to strike another blow. Horrified, Claire blurted, “May I help you?”

A man twisted around to look, and she sucked in a breath so hard she felt it reach her toes. He fanned the cloud of plaster in the air and stumbled down the ladder, almost landing in a pile at her feet. Instead, he caught himself on the counter with a tanned hand and splayed fingers. Round, dark eyes in a long face glimmered with interest. One or two loose strands of silver highlighted his hairline at the temples. She stared in surprise.

He dusted himself off then shot her another look laced with curiosity. “Can I help *you*?” His voice had a deep Southern drawl that made him sound like a sheriff. Something about him was familiar although she was sure she wouldn’t have forgotten him if she’d met him before.

“Well…this is my house,” Claire explained, feeling her cheeks warm and wondering why she was blushing. Was this the Realtor from Coates and Coburn she’d spoken with six weeks ago?

The man studied her as if she were making it up. "You're the owner?" he mused in a tone mingled with doubt. "I didn't know Miss Henny personally, but I'm pretty sure you're not family."

Claire stiffened. Just because she was fair didn't mean beautiful, dark-skinned Miss Henny could not have been family. "I'm her..." Claire wavered before saying "foster daughter" and explaining the whole story. Not many people would remember her except for a few neighbors or older members of the local church congregation. She'd kept to herself in school. "I'm Claire Woodbury."

"Are you the one selling the house?"

Claire gave her head a small shake. "I was, but I changed my mind and decided to move in." She didn't mention her apartment roommate had asked her and Emily to leave. A toddler had been too much, but it was fine because Miss Henny had left Claire the house in Georgia. Emily and she didn't have a lot, but they had each other.

The stranger's jaw softened and it made him look crestfallen over the news.

"So why are you here then?" Claire tried to sound friendly and not suspicious.

"You're not selling." The man's face clouded. "But I thought—"

"No." She bit her lip, oddly disheartened to be disappointing him.

He looked up at the holes he'd punched into the ceiling. She could have sworn his cheeks reddened. "Leaks," he explained with an upward motion. "There's insect damage outside the window, and there's been a leak, too."

Claire realized the ceiling tiles were stained in several different spots. Her enthusiasm for renovations took another swan dive. "The roof's leaking and there're termites?"

"I think so." The man dusted himself off and offered a hand. "Bradley." His hand looked friendly, and his muscled arm was…

"Claire," Claire repeated, and their fingers tangled in an awkward clasp. He grinned like he didn't feel a tingle shoot up his arm the way she did. It forced a dimple into one of his tanned cheeks. She jerked herself back to attention and returned to his steady gaze that reminded her of milk chocolate.

"This is going to cost a pretty penny," he warned. A light five-o'-clock shadow on his chin made him look like a rascal.

At least Claire tried to think of him that way and ignore the fact his dark good looks and boyish dimple made her heart skip at first glance. Her heart was still skipping, she realized with dismay. She forced herself to think about pennies instead.

Henny House was looking more and more expensive, and she needed a roof over her head. That meant the pottery studio would have to wait, although she had to have it if she was going to create a comfortable and secure life for Emily. Suddenly her throat swelled with remnants of grief. She'd made it to Miss Henny's funeral but not the house, because she'd had to get back to Emily and to work. Ms. Olivia had taken care of locking up, but Claire had never imagined that Henny House would fall into disrepair in such a short time.

She eyed the stranger and tried to hide her surprise

and growing unease. The first thing she needed to do was to get him out of her new home.

Bradley Ainsworth realized he was staring at the pint-sized woman who'd snatched away his ticket to a position on the local historical preservation board. "I'm sorry. I didn't mean to scare you," he insisted, reminding himself not to ramble like he did when caught off guard. "I work with Parker and Associates Construction and viewed the house a couple months ago. I've always admired it, so I decided to come over for another look before making an offer."

Brushing slanted bangs behind her ear, he watched Claire Woodbury swallow before looking him straight in the eye. "Well, I'm Miss Henny's heir, I guess you could say. I lived with her until I graduated high school. She was the only real mother I ever had, although it was only for a few years."

"She must have appreciated that."

"I always kept in touch with her," Claire assured him. "I loved her. Stray cats, dogs and wounded birds all found a home here. So did kids from the state foster system." Her face reddened.

Bradley thought he had detected cats but didn't mention the odor. He hadn't known the previous owner had been a foster parent.

Claire looked at the fresh holes in the ceiling, and Bradley knew he would have to fix them whether he bought Henny House from her or not. She likely had a long renovation list by the looks of things. He crinkled his forehead with feeble hope. "So will you sell this place after you fix it up?"

"No, I intend to settle here for good."

Bradley felt his face cloud with emotion at her reply. He reminded himself that Henny House was hers, and he should accept it even if she was as charming and attractive as she was determined, but he couldn't resist. "I'd still like to make you an offer. This house will be a lot of work, and it needs to be done right."

Claire raised a brow. "Yes, but I have plans to completely gut this wonder and bring it into the modern age. New drywall, new floors, and that's just for starters. The weird gazebo on the porch will definitely go, and the exterior needs a coat of fresh paint."

"Not the gazebo." Bradley cringed at the thought. The little imp had the nerve to smile at him. "What color paint?" he asked with trepidation.

"Eggplant," she announced.

His mouth wrenched in horror. "Are you sure I can't buy it from you?" he blurted.

"I'm sorry, no." An apologetic frown touched Claire's lips. "I didn't realize anyone wanted it so badly."

Bradley took a resolute breath. "I restore and sell properties for the company I work for, and like I said, I've always wondered about this place. It's different. Quirky. Being a contractor, I want to return it to its original glory—which means no new flooring or purple paint."

"Eggplant," Claire corrected him. "You're a contractor?"

"Yes, for historical homes. Did you know the local historical preservation board would love to see this house restored?" Bradley folded his arms, hoping he looked like a world-renowned expert and forced himself not to cross his fingers. "How much would it take to convince you to sell, Claire? Why don't you give me a number, and I'll see what I can do?"

She examined him, taking in his watch and shoes, and he detected a hint of disdain. It made him flush, and he wished he'd worn his work clothes instead of coming straight over from the office.

"Are you sure this is about preservation?" she asked. "How do I know you're not some real estate tycoon that wants to buy the house to convert it to your taste then sell it to make a few bucks?"

A laugh of surprise escaped him. Bradley shook his head in wonder. "I just like to hang on to old things and keep them special. Name your price." The woman was protective of the house, he'd give her that much, and if she'd grown up without any family except for Miss Henny, it was no wonder she'd come back to Kudzu Creek. Georgia had certainly called him home.

"Again, I'm sorry. I don't have a price," said Claire. "I just moved here and I intend to live in Kudzu Creek in this house. I'll fix it up as I go along."

"By yourself?"

"I'm pretty handy, believe it or not, and what I can't do myself, I'll hire out." Claire met his eyes with confidence. "I had practice repairing things in some of my not-so-extravagant homes growing up, plus I've been watching do-it-yourself videos."

Bradley choked down a laugh and scratched his neck to disguise his frustration.

Claire offered her hand again. "I am glad to meet you. It's been a long time since I've lived here, and I really don't know anyone."

He accepted her hand, and it felt as warm and inviting as the first time.

"Nice to meet you then." He surrendered with what he hoped was an alluring smile. "I'll call the real estate company and let them know they forgot to inform me the house is no longer available."

"Thank you." Claire seemed to be warming up to him despite his disappointment. Maybe there was still room to change her mind.

"I don't mean to get into your business—" Bradley hounded her in one last desperate effort "—but are you sure you want to modernize this place? It's so unique, and since it was built in the 1890s it'd be amazing to restore it to how it originally looked."

"I'm an artist," Claire explained, "a ceramist, and Miss Henny always loved things that were modern and funky. She'd be excited."

A good-humored expression at her defensive excuse slid off Bradley's face when a small child who captured his attention toddled up beside her.

"Ca-re?"

Claire looked down as the little girl grabbed the side of her slacks with one hand and stuck a thumb in her mouth with the other. Her innocent coffee-brown glance gave Bradley a penetrating once-over.

"Hi there." He shifted his gaze back to Claire, trying to hide his surprise.

She picked up the toddler and rested her on her hip. "This is my girl Emily. She's going to live here, too, and we're going to build a pottery studio once we get this house up to speed."

"I see." Bradley's cheeks warmed for some strange reason. "I didn't realize you had a family." He hurried across the room for his cell phone and cluster of keys. "I should go. I was just on my way to another project and—" He glanced back at Emily then took a card from his shirt pocket and tossed it on the counter. "My business card," he explained. He gave Claire and the child a small wave. "Just in case you change your mind about selling the house." He left through the mudroom, head spinning, after a promise to return to patch up the ceiling.

Striding down the driveway, Bradley knew the tepid morning would be as muggy as a damp sweater by lunchtime so he maintained his pace as he marched down the road back to the office on Creek Street. They were expecting him at the Monroe project.

Ducking under branches of fuchsia-colored crepe myrtle blooms, Bradley fought an urge to look back over his shoulder at Henny House as his heart bounced around in his chest. He knew it was from the encounter with Miss Henny's heiress more than the strenuous stride back to work. His offer to buy the house couldn't have gone any worse.

His neck grew damp, and Bradley swiped at it. It left grit from the Henny House ceiling tiles clinging to his fingers. He grunted in self-reproach. The toddler had startled him, too. Her brilliant white-blond hair and dark eyes reminded him of someone he knew, but he couldn't think of whom. He'd been so busy trying to figure out who the interesting new homeowner was, he hadn't stopped to consider she might be married with a child. The whole encounter had left him completely unsettled and he'd bolted.

Chagrined, he reached the corner of Maple Grove Lane and waved at a car rolling by to mask his snarled emotions. Losing the purchase of Henny House meant he couldn't keep his word to the historical preservation board that he could restore it to its former grandeur. Bradley's stomach sank. Since dropping out of a masters of accounting program and running off to California with his childhood sweetheart, his parents had considered him a rebel. Coming home divorced and without a higher degree a few years later, they now treated him like a thirty-one-year-old failure.

He wanted that house. He *needed* to get on the board. It was the only thing that would prove to his parents he was serious about his new life and career since moving back to Georgia. He could be successful renovating historic homes here and someday have a respected and profitable business. All he needed was a chance.

Bradley hurried across Creek Street's cobblestones to the other side and walked to the office of Parker and Associates. His new-to-him, slightly used truck was parked at an angle out front.

He checked his phone once settled inside. The plumber from the Monroe project had left a message, and his cousin, Donovan, had called twice. Bradley zipped out of the parking spot but drove the low speed limit with restraint down Creek Street until it became the highway. Set free, he pressed the gas pedal halfway to the floor, his mind trying to focus on today's to-do list for the Monroe's master bath while his heart tripped along uneasily, stressing over the Henny House fiasco.

Chapter Two

Claire couldn't resist peeking out the window as Mr. Thu dug around his giant elephant ear plants next door. It helped distract her from thinking about the contractor who'd been in her house the day before. Mr. Thu's tropical foliage made an unusual border between the two yards. She'd recognized him immediately and couldn't stop thinking about the old days while she'd scrubbed down the kitchen. At least it would be sanitary enough to eat in even if it looked derelict.

She dropped down onto the floor with Emily and shared a banana and crusty cereal bar. "Do you want to play outside?"

Emily mushed a bite of banana into the back of her mouth. "Out," she agreed.

Claire allowed herself a smile. Emily had all the room in the world to play now. Having a yard would be a big change and a lot of work, but it was wonderful for an active toddler. The house was another thing entirely. There was so much more damage than she'd expected… And the contractor? What a stubborn man. She wouldn't change her mind. She'd watched his retreating silhouette until it banged out onto the back porch and disappeared. Unconcerned, Emily had scurried across the room to explore the kitchen cabinets with childlike curiosity.

Curious indeed. Claire wondered if Bradley had walked to the property from his place of employment and puzzled over why he wanted the house so badly. She needed it more. She needed to open a pottery studio so she could be a stay-at-home parent, and most of all, for once in her thirty years, she wanted to know what it was like to have a permanent address.

Remembering the business card Bradley had casually given her, Claire climbed up from the floor and searched the counter. There. She'd forgotten he'd left it. She picked it up with interest. It was an unusual peach-pink color with the brown outline of a typical Victorian-era home. Across the top in calligraphy was stamped *Parker and Associates Construction.* Underneath were two lines in a plain font: Bradley Ainsworth. Historical Properties Specialist.

Ainsworth. Now there was a name she'd heard before. Claire tapped the card on the counter. She was going to need a contractor at some point, but handsome or not, a historical preservationist with a bias against purple paint was not the right man for the job.

Emily climbed up with sandaled feet and clapped her hands. "Outside!" she insisted.

Claire laughed, dodging the two sticky little hands that reached out to cup her knee. A glimmer of Dori's good humor sparkled in her daughter's smile. "Okay, sweet girl. Let's wash our hands and go outside and play."

Claire helped Emily navigate three big steps to the small patio after leading her through the mudroom. She kept an eye on the side yard should Mr. Thu look her way. He probably wouldn't recognize her after all this time. Did he know Miss Henny had left her the house? He'd only spoken to Claire back and forth over the elephant ear plants a few times through the years, but he'd helped Miss Henny with leaky faucets and went to her church. They'd been old friends. Claire wondered if he knew Bradley Ainsworth.

The sunshine sparkling off a generous-sized metal shed in the backyard distracted her from any more questions, and she put her hands on her hips and examined it. There would be no extra money to build a brand-new studio on a property with a roof to replace, so she needed a solution. Her ceramics business was the only plan she had to provide for Emily if she wanted to work from home and not put the little girl in childcare.

The shed's white paint was peeling and one of the double doors looked like it had a loose hinge. Clutter was stacked to the windows whose cobwebs testified that no one had cleaned it out since she'd last lived here. Claire frowned. Her own art space was a must. With a few contacts in Atlanta and several online shops that had already purchased some of her pottery, she didn't want to lose her momentum.

Claire checked and saw Emily talking to herself from astride her new pink trike on the patio. Pushing back a dread of spiders, she unlatched the rusty lock of the shed and pulled open one of the whining doors with trepidation. Shafts of sunlight pierced an assortment of yard equipment, outdoor chairs and umbrellas. Claire scanned the back wall and saw her old boogie board for the beach. There were two bicycles. One had been hers, although it no longer looked like it would stay together if she climbed onto it. The air smelled like dust and oil.

Something buzzed in the corner. She looked up at the soft but foreboding sound. There was a generous wasp nest, too. "Oh, no," she groaned. The shed was in terrible condition and no way near ready to become a makeshift studio. She stepped out to avoid riling anything up and glanced back at Emily. To her surprise, Mr. Thu, having crossed the barrier between their properties, was now crouching in front of the trike. The older man and child were having an animated conversation about the rainbow-streaked pony on Emily's shirt. Her teeny finger pointed at the glittery mane.

"Hello, Mr. Thu." Claire bit her lip to keep a sheepish smile at bay. The small man, balder and thinner than she remembered, crawled to his feet with some effort and wiped his hands on his dark green trousers. "Why, Claire Henny. You're all grown up."

She laughed. "It's Claire Woodbury," she reminded him, "but sometimes I felt like a Henny, although she never adopted me." Claire held out her hand, and Mr. Thu pulled her in for a half-embrace and patted her elbow. "Ms. Olivia down the street told me Miss Henny left you this place. I'm glad to see you're back home."

"Yes, Ms. Olivia's been keeping an eye on it, and I'm happy to be here."

"So are you selling or not?"

Claire hesitated, her mind seeing Bradley on the stepladder in the kitchen with his foreboding report. "I hope I'm here for good."

Her next door neighbor's face brightened. "That's wonderful news."

"I'm glad you think so. I know it needs a lot of work, but Emily and I are up to the challenge."

"Oh, Emily it is it? All I could get out of her was to see the pony."

Claire laughed. "She's definitely a horse girl and loves to be outside."

"Well, you have a nice yard here." Mr. Thu was gracious and said nothing about the tall weeds and untrimmed trees.

"I know it's a lot of work," Claire began, "but…"

"There are people who can help you."

"Yes," she agreed. "Miss Henny left some funds for that." She thought of Bradley Ainsworth. "As a matter of fact, a man from Parker and Associates was here yesterday. He was interested in buying the house, and I understand he does renovation as well."

"Ainsworth? Oh, yes," remarked Mr. Thu. "Ms. Olivia said she saw him walking around before your car showed up. That'd be Ainsworth's nephew. Harold Ainsworth from the bank. His nephew moved back from California a while ago I hear. Many people recommend him." Mr. Thu glanced overhead as if searching for a memory in the trees. "He used to run with Ainsworth's son when he would visit from Lake Charles way back when. They're one of the old families. Have all that land in the county. Do you remember them?"

Claire smiled but shrugged helplessly. Her mind scrambled for details. It'd been so long ago, she could hardly remember, and it wasn't like she'd made a lot of friends being Miss Henny's ward. Mr. Thu pointed at the shed. "Are you looking for something?"

"Oh, no," chuckled Claire. She waved a hand as if introducing him to it. "I hoped I could use this space as a pottery studio, but I need to get it cleaned out and figure out a way to run electricity inside."

"Now that's a chore," the gentleman said. "I can help you get things sorted out, but I'm no electrician."

"You don't have to do that."

Mr. Thu grinned. "Now, Claire, with my Marilee gone and Miss Henny, too, who else am I going to take care of around here? You go play with Emily and let me get started with some of that old stuff."

"There's wasps."

"They don't scare me. I can take care of the grass and fire ants in the front, and do this to keep your little girl safe. Let me help."

Claire's heart swelled with gratitude. Perhaps setting up a studio in the old shed wouldn't be impossible after all. "Thank you, Mr. Thu, but just this once. I'm going to owe you big-time."

Striding toward the office Friday morning, Bradley saw Southern Fried Kudzu had vacant tables outside and wondered if he had time to grab breakfast. His boss wasn't expecting him for another half hour. He glanced through the plate-glass window of Parker and Associates, lowered his head and made a run for it.

Two doors down, the eatery offered coffee and biscuits in the mornings, along with a glass case heaped with tarts. Bradley eased inside and inhaled the welcoming scent of ground coffee beans as he tried to push Henny House from his mind. He'd tossed and turned all week.

He wanted it badly. To take the town eyesore and turn it into the beauty it'd once been made his mouth water. Even though he'd made his interest in the historical preservation board's vacancy clear, the old-timers weren't sure of him. He'd only been in town over a year, so he wasn't one of the good ol' boys…yet.

The diner hummed with cheerful morning conversations. Bradley followed the fragrance of mouthwatering food to the counter. He was so intent on the goodies in the glass case he didn't recognize the back of his cousin at the register.

Donovan Ainsworth surprised him when he turned around, a steaming paper cup raised to his lips. "What are you doing here?"

Bradley straightened from examining the baked goods. "I was on my way into the office and thought I smelled doughnuts."

Donovan glanced at the display case. "She has strawberry-kiwi tarts if you don't want a sausage biscuit."

Bradley rubbed his lips together, and his stomach rumbled. "Don't let Aunt Vi catch you here again," he warned. Donovan lived in his aunt and uncle's guesthouse and usually ate his mother's cooking at her insistence.

He shrugged. "I have an early case this morning."

"I guess that's a good excuse. Hope it goes well." Bradley felt no ill will toward his cousin, who'd chosen law after Bradley had refused to consider it like his parents had first hoped. They'd decided accounting was the next best thing for him, but he'd eventually rebelled against that, too.

"How's the fixer-upper business?" Donovan motioned toward an available table, and Bradley decided it'd be better to eat inside so no one from the office saw him loitering. He raised a finger to ask for a moment and made his order at the register. "Two tarts and a chocolate milk with ice."

McKenzie, better known as Mac, gave him a quick nod. It was always chocolate milk. He turned to the small table and joined his cousin. "What's the case today?"

Donovan made a noncommittal noise. He never talked about his clients or their cases. He wasn't judgmental and didn't gossip. Bradley admired him for it. It was more than he could say about a lot of people he knew. Donovan blew over the top of his steaming drink and set it down. "How about you? Did you finish the Monroe project?"

"Everything except the master bath." Bradley leaned forward. "We're going to repair the original tiles and put in a soaker tub—a replica since the one in there now is fiberglass."

His cousin grinned. "Who knew you'd run off to San Francisco and come home with Grandma Shirley's taste?"

Trying not to wince at the mention of the West Coast where he'd let down his family, Bradley replied, "You might have, too. No one can help but love the history and architecture. I moved out there to get a job working in those grand houses, and it was a dream of a lifetime."

"And to woo Dori," Donovan reminded him.

Bradley grimaced but lifted his chin in quiet acknowledgment. It was hard to explain to people how he'd changed after foolishly eloping to California with his lifelong best friend.

And Dori Rochester had quickly changed her mind. Realizing their friendship could never be anything more and stung by her parents' threats to cut her off, she'd asked for an annulment and returned to Georgia after only two months with him. Bradley had stayed and learned to appreciate what mattered most. He'd even started going back to church. It was a slice of humble pie he never wanted to taste again.

Donovan unfolded a napkin and shook it out. "I'm glad you moved to Kudzu Creek instead of back to Lake Charles. There's been no one to hang out with or listen to me complain."

"Just like the old days." Bradley smiled, although both of them were so busy neither one had much free time. "Moving back to Lake Charles near Mom and Dad didn't feel right," Bradley admitted, not to mention the cold reception he knew he'd receive after quitting his master's program before eloping with and then divorcing Dori. "I appreciate Aunt Vi's invitation and your dad's reference for the Parker and Associates' job. Now I just need the historical preservation board appointment, and maybe my folks will relax and quit worrying about me."

Donovan made a small noise of approval before taking a bite out of a biscuit. "I know you're trying to make things right with them and still have the career you want. It's impressive how much you've accomplished since those summer jobs in construction. I bet your parents regret making you work as soon as you turned fourteen, even if it was part-time."

Bradley stared down at the table. "They just regret I didn't go into law or become an accountant."

Donovan elbowed him. "Don't worry about the historical committee. You're overqualified."

Bradley gave a modest, slight nod. His cousin had seen the portfolio of homes he'd helped restore in San

Francisco, so he hoped Donovan was right. Having a town appointment along with his job at the elite Parker and Associates would help his family see he'd not only matured but could make a living doing what he loved. Restoring Henny House had been his ticket to showing everyone he was a changed and successful man, even if he'd failed at marriage.

Mac appeared with his tarts and milk. "Thanks," Bradley murmured, and she patted him on the shoulder. He bit into a warm tart. The drizzled icing melted in his mouth while he ignored the painful idea of Henny House no longer being for sale. "I met one of old Miss Henny's foster children from years ago."

His cousin's brows shot up with interest.

"She has a family," Bradley informed him, smacking sugar off his lips, "and they've moved into Henny House."

"I thought you were going to buy it."

"I was." Bradley swiped at a crumb. "I went over the other day to figure out how much would be a fair offer, and she was there. She's decided not to sell it, and they're moving in."

"What's her name?"

"Claire Woodbury."

Donovan wrinkled his forehead. "I don't remember her, but I went to the county high school. That's too bad about the house."

Bradley grunted in frustrated agreement.

"It'll work out. You deserve it." Donovan gave him an encouraging nod. "You found a lot more than your future career out there in California."

Bradley lifted his chin. "If you mean my faith, you're right, because if I'm going to go to church, I'm going to mean it. Just like if I tear down a house—I'll build it back up the way it was meant to be."

Donovan searched the street through the plate-glass front window. "Now you can make Kudzu Creek as pretty as you did the City by the Bay." Donovan's joshing hinted at respect.

"I should get to work." Bradley sighed.

Donovan wiped at his mouth with a napkin. "I need to head to the courthouse. Are you coming for Sunday supper?"

"Maybe. I want to try to sort out this Henny House problem."

"Just offer her some money," Donovan suggested.

"I did," Bradley admitted. "She refused." He felt his cheeks warm with mild shame that he'd tried throwing money at her. It was something his parents would have done. "Her husband wasn't there, so maybe I can talk him into it when I meet him." Bradley pushed back from the table with renewed determination. "I need that house, Donovan. It's one of the oldest homes still standing in Kudzu Creek, and there's no way they'll refuse my application to the board if I restore it. I'd be their hero."

"Then convince the new owners to let you do just a few things," Donovan suggested. "It sure needs it."

It'd crossed his mind until the mention of pulling up wood floors and, for heaven's sake, destroying the gazebo. Bradley rubbed his chin. "You're right. I need to find a way to convince them to preserve as much of the house as possible and let me do it. If I can get them to see my vision, perhaps Claire would change her mind after all."

"If anyone can do it, Brad Bo Ainsworth can," Donovan praised.

Bradley snorted. Brad Bo? He hadn't been called by his high school nickname in years, but his heart rose as his cousin said goodbye and charged out of the diner. Could he really pull it off?

See you next summer, Brad Bo! Dori would have cheered him on. She'd always called him Brad, even after he'd gone off to college in Athens and started going by his full name.

Bradley caught himself working his jaw as he hurried out to get to work. *Stop*, he chided himself. He'd moved on and was better for it. In his heart, he had to believe Dori had made peace with him.

He allowed a small, sad sigh. Dori and he were the one thing he'd never be able to restore, no matter how many houses he fixed up. Their friendship could never be repaired because she was gone now. Instead, he'd have to concentrate on preserving his aunt and uncle's hometown that he loved so much. And he'd start with Henny House. Somehow.

Bradley returned to the office after a few hours at the Monroe project and filed some paperwork. Not hungry for any lunch, he ambled through town then crossed the street to Maple Grove Lane like he was just out for a stroll. In the distance, he saw that the For Sale sign had been removed from the Henny House yard and trash was piled on the curb. He made his way down the sidewalk to the front yard of the house and realized the grass had been cut, too. It looked nice.

"Excuse me!"

Bradley looked over his shoulder and saw an elderly

woman across the street. She waved him over, and he exhaled at the interruption. She stood no more than knee high to a June bug, as his uncle would say, but there was an urgency about her expression, as if she had something very important to tell him. Afraid she would stumble into the middle of the road, Bradley raised a hand in acknowledgment and jogged over.

"Hello." She grinned with small teeth too perfect to be real. "Do you remember me?"

Bradley's mind raced, but he recovered nothing. "No, ma'am, I don't."

"Why, you used to come to my house selling school fundraisers," she chided him, "with your adorable cousin."

"Donovan?"

"Yes, Donovan. I know your Aunt Vi. We serve together on the church welcome committee."

"It's very nice to see you again, Mrs...." Bradley gave her a helpless smile. "I'm sorry, I—"

"Ms. Olivia," she prompted him. "Mrs. Olivia Cleveland. You remember?"

"That's right. I'm sorry," Bradley apologized. He realized her dark short hair was a little too perfect and a peculiar shape that reminded him of a hairpiece.

"Well, I just wanted you to know that someone has already moved into that place." She pointed back across the street. "Poor Miss Henny had a stroke not too long ago, and I've been watching the house."

"That's so kind of you," Bradley replied. He tried not to glance at his watch. "I have met the new homeowner already. I was just checking in."

"Oh, you have then?" Ms. Olivia gave him a wink. "I just wanted to make sure. Can't have strangers wandering around Maple Grove Lane," she teased. "Not that you're a stranger."

He chuckled. "I like to think not. I do renovations for Parker and Associates, and I'm looking into Henny House as a project."

Ms. Olivia's faint brows rose. "Oh, that's right. I heard you were doing the Monroe house, and a fine job, too."

Bradley wondered if there was anything Ms. Olivia did not know. "That's right. Well," he said in a quick breath, "I should get over there before my lunch break is over."

She beamed. "It's so good of you to check on Miss Henny's ward. Did you know she has a baby?"

"Yes, I've seen her," said Bradley. He stepped off the curb. "I guess I'll talk to you soon, Ms. Olivia."

"I'm sure you will if you're going to be working on this house," she declared.

He smiled at her. "I don't have the job yet."

The woman put a tiny hand on her crooked waist. "Oh, you will," she assured him. "I'll put in a good word for you, and my word's as good as gold."

Thanking her, Bradley hurried across the street before he was distracted with any more questions. Striding up onto the front porch, he rapped on the door: no footsteps, no voices. Remembering the kitchen in the back, he wandered around the wraparound porch, noting it had been swept clean.

He found Claire and her little girl in their backyard. The trilling sounds of childish giggles rippled through the air as they chased bubbles shooting out from some kind of bubble machine. "They didn't have stuff like that when we were kids." Bradley stopped on the last step and put his hands on his hips.

The petite blonde with the short, pixie-like hairstyle straightened with a surprised look on her face. "No, they didn't."

"I thought I would check back in with you," explained Bradley. "How are things? Is your husband in town?"

Claire stilled like a deer for several seconds, staring at him with bright eyes. "I'm not married," she informed him. Her cheeks turned as pink as carnations. Leaving the baby to her giggles, Claire suddenly strode toward Bradley, wiping her hands off on her jeans. "Actually it's probably good you're here," she said. "I almost emailed you this morning with a question."

Bradley felt something like interest sprout wings. She wasn't married, and she'd thought about contacting him. She had a kid, and he loved kids. "You've changed your mind?"

"No, and I'm sorry." Claire gave him an apologetic smile. "I need an outlet in the shed back here as soon as possible," she explained, "and I thought you could recommend someone." She held up her palms in surrender. "I've searched local electricians online, but I'm lost."

Bradley did his best to hide his disappointment. "I suppose I could send you a few names, but it is in my wheelhouse. I could do it if you want." He folded his arms and tried to look casual. "So you and your daughter live alone?"

"Emily is not actually my daughter. I'm her guardian." Claire glanced back at the child chasing bubbles with delight, and another soft smile touched her lips.

"That's pretty special. It sounds like something Miss Henny would have done from what I've heard of her."

"It is," Claire agreed, "and it's the least I can do, considering what other folks have done for me."

Bradley caught himself looking Claire up and down. Did she have a significant other? "So about this electrical outlet..." he prodded as a clever idea crept into his mind. "Where do you need it?" If he could put in an outlet, maybe that would lead to more involvement in the renovation, and he could convince her to save the gazebo and restore, rather than annihilate, the rest of the house. Not to mention, he suspected he'd enjoy her company.

Claire looped a thumb over her shoulder toward a storage shed that had seen better days. "In that thing."

"Want me to take a look?"

"All right." She headed up the sloping yard, and Bradley followed.

He felt a stab of guilt for wanting to steal the house out from under her. He liked her. She seemed fun and obviously had a lot of love to give. His heart suddenly felt as gooey as one of Mac's fruit tarts. Glancing over at Emily dancing in the grass to some unheard song, he followed Claire up to the shed with a small chuckle at the little girl's antics. Claire's back was to him, and he found himself admiring the curve of her neck until he tripped over the threshold.

"See?" Claire ignored his clumsy stumble. Her tone was all businesslike. "It's just an old storage shed but it does have windows for ventilation and a plywood floor. My neighbor helped me clean it out, and I can put in a portable sink. I just need electricity for my kiln."

Bradley looked around the space with approval. Two

windows at either end had been washed clean to let in more light. There was a work table with lower cabinets pushed against a wall, and a few heavy boxes and paintings of horses and cows were stacked on the floor. "Did you paint these?" He couldn't resist walking over to examine them.

"Yes, I'm going to hang them up in here."

"They're nice." To be friendly, Bradley crouched and thumbed through them. A few framed photographs fell over beside the paintings and he picked one up and studied it with interest. "Is this you?"

Claire moved beside him and picked up some of the fallen frames. "Yes, the first month I lived with Miss Henny."

"You haven't changed all that much," Bradley noted. In the picture, a younger version of Claire with long hair stood shoulder to shoulder by a round lady with dark skin and shining curls that he assumed was Miss Henny. Claire's smile looked timid. Miss Henny's smile stretched ear to ear and glowed like the moon. Bradley couldn't resist examining another photograph—a baby picture that looked like Emily. "She's beautiful," he said.

"She is." Claire reached for it and the other pictures in her grip clattered to the floor. Bradley tried to catch them, but the last one made him fall back on his heels. He picked it up as shock coursed through him. "Hey, this looks like—this is—"

Claire cradled it in her arms. "This is Emily's mother. I mean, it was. She was a dear friend, and I promised myself I'd raise her daughter for her and give her a happy life."

Mind whirling, Bradley lowered himself to the floor

and sat cross-legged beside the boxes. "Can I look at it again?" He held out an insistent hand and, after a long pause, Claire passed it over, but she didn't sit beside him. Her wide eyes looked as surprised as he felt.

He studied the picture with a galloping heart. Long fair hair parted down the middle. Intelligent smile. Bright blue eyes. Dori Rochester. His childhood sweetheart. His summer partner in crime. His unexpected and whirlwind romance—and marriage. Of course, Emily was hers. He didn't need to look outside to see the resemblance between the baby and Dori. He couldn't tear his eyes away. "This was a yearbook picture," he murmured.

There was a long silence.

Bradley looked up, clutching the picture in his hands.

"It was." Claire stepped back. Her voice sounded thick.

"I'm sorry." He pushed to his feet, hoping to break the spell. "I should explain that I knew her. I grew up around here, a few miles away in Lake Charles." His brow furrowed.

"How did you know her?" he wondered suddenly. "We were best friends when we were kids, but she was from Albany."

Claire's throat rippled with a silent swallow. "Dori and I were roommates in college at the University of Alabama at Birmingham. Later, she lived with me until..."

Bradley felt his shoulders droop. "She passed." He nodded in understanding at Claire's sadness. "I heard."

Dori had quit speaking to him, but his mother had heard she'd died in an accident somewhere around Birmingham. It had only taken a few minutes of searching social media to see if it was true. Dori's parents had never bothered to let him know about or even invite him to the funeral. Was it because she'd gone on to have a child? And whose was she?

Claire looked confused. Did she know what had happened between Dori and him? Bradley felt his face warm with mild embarrassment and set the picture back on the floor.

"I better check on Emily. It's her naptime." Claire backed away a few steps then strode out of the shed.

Bradley followed. She obviously didn't want to talk about it, and he understood. Grief was a hard, persistent thing, but he found it touching that Claire had once lived in Kudzu Creek then met Dori all the way over in Alabama. But what on earth had Dori said about him?

"Hey!" he called, determined to win her over, "I can run that electricity for you to the shed if you want me to. It'd be no problem." She didn't respond, and he felt awful he'd stirred up some grief. She'd not only lost Miss Henny, she'd lost Dori a couple of years back, too. So had he. The old wound in his chipped heart pulsated.

Claire turned to face him with a hand resting on Emily's shoulder. The little girl was sitting on the porch steps plucking a white dandelion into pieces. "I don't need the electricity right now," Claire replied, "but I will later. You said you could give me some names for the roof?"

Bradley nodded. "Sure. In fact, if you're looking for a contractor to manage the whole project, I'd be happy to volunteer."

She pressed her lips together as if considering it. He raised his hands in defeat. "I know you aren't interested in preserving everything, so we'll do it your way, except for the gazebo. You'll have to compromise on that because I may not have the heart to remove it." The historical preservation board would be up in arms if that happened.

Claire scooped Emily into her arms. "It's not a bad idea, but I'm not sure the gazebo is up for debate. I'll have to get back to you later. It's time for this little one's nap."

Bradley studied the darling toddler, and something pricked the back of his mind. How old was she? She grinned back at him. He realized Claire was waiting on him to leave. Talking about Dori had seemed to ruin her morning. "Fine. I'll come by again in a couple days to run the electricity, and we can talk about the roofing references."

"See you then." She gave him a tight smile and disappeared inside the house with the faint sounds of Emily announcing it was time for snacks rather than naptime.

Bradley took an unsteady step toward the crumbling driveway. His heart felt like a fist had punched him in the breastbone. Being hired to help fix up Henny House was a good thing, but working with one of Dori's best friends could be a problem. He was trying to move on and pretend his marriage and annulment had never happened, or at least make everyone else forget it. He wondered how much Dori had confided in Claire. She'd definitely acted surprised and uncomfortable. And the little girl? Where was her father?

His stomach felt sick at the thought of pursuing that question, but he found enough strength to jog down the driveway and head to the office. The pounding of his footfalls echoed in his head the entire way. *Do-ri. Do-ri. Do-ri.*

Chapter Three

Claire knew it was rude to disappear into the house, but her brain was cloudy. For some reason, her arms and legs felt unsteady, too. Clutching Emily, she made a beeline for the bedroom they were sharing for now, shut the door and sat on the floor. She needed a contractor. Bradley wasn't a perfect fit, though he'd do. But he knew Dori? Emily poised herself on a little pink rug, her eyes wide in confusion. Even she knew snacks came before naptime. "Snack?" she pleaded.

Claire put a hand to her chest to try to stop her racing pulse. This should have been good news, something special, but it didn't feel right. Her heart squeezed. Brad Bo? Brad Bo Ainsworth. What little Dori had told her about Emily's father hadn't really stuck, but she knew his name was Brad. "It's time to go night-night, Emily." The little girl's lips puckered. "I'll get you a drink."

Ignoring her own dry throat, Claire dashed to the kitchen, filled a sippy cup with water and hurried back to the bedroom. Emily had pulled herself up onto the double bed in the room and was hopping around in circles.

Claire helped her drink, changed her diaper and then convinced her to lie down with a favorite blanket. She sang a few nursery rhymes to get the child's mind off snacks, and finally, Emily curled her back up against Claire's midriff and floated off to sleep.

The gentle fragrance of lavender perfumed the little girl's hair, and inhaling it relaxed a pinch in Claire's shoulders. She let her eyes blink shut and allowed the echo of Emily's heartbeat to calm her own. Having an angel in her life to show her the wonder of the world through innocent eyes had changed her. Emily loved her unconditionally, and Claire knew she'd walk through fire for her even if…

A nauseating feeling washed over her, and the pinch in her heart rose to her throat with a feeling of panic. *Ainsworth.* The name Dori had decided not to put on Emily's birth certificate. No wonder it had rung a bell. Bradley Ainsworth knew Dori. Could Brad Bo Ainsworth and Bradley Ainsworth be one and the same?

The painful knot tied itself in Claire's throat. Bradley and Dori were from the same area. Bradley's brown-eyed stare hovered in her mind and then, from out of nowhere, a hot rush of fear washed over her.

If it were true, she could lose Emily. The knot in her throat turned to pain.

Claire had never been able to hold on to what mattered most when life flipped the pages. Homes left behind. Families forgotten. People passing through her life year after year like disposable figurines. And just when she'd managed to get her feet back on the ground, another disaster.

Perhaps she'd known it as soon as she'd picked up the business card. It'd been easier to believe Bradley was a good-looking, overconfident real estate investor who liked to play handyman rather than Dori's childhood best friend she'd heard about. What was Bradley doing in Kudzu Creek? Had his relationship with the West Coast ended, too?

Claire wiped a fugitive tear from her eye, her grief over Dori raw. With a heavy sigh, she forced herself out of bed and eased from the room. In the parlor, she flopped down onto a faded velvet chaise and opened her laptop.

"Oh, Miss Henny," she choked, "if only you were here. I need you today." She swiped her long bangs out of her eyes as she searched the internet for the Ainsworth family of Lake Charles. The results nearly cracked her numb heart into icicles. It was true. His father was once mayor. His mother had several mentions with the chamber of commerce. Even Bradley had newspaper articles that congratulated him for winning debates on his private school's debate team.

Claire swallowed the panic and snapped the laptop shut. All of the problems with the house and pottery business shifted into the background. She'd promised Emily, sworn to her, that she would take care of her as Dori would have if she'd lived. Now what? Emily's father was most likely alive and well and living in Kudzu Creek, and he had a right to know about his little girl.

Bradley caught himself looking over his shoulder for Claire Woodbury and the baby at church on Sunday, but they were nowhere to be seen. Maybe Claire didn't go to church, or maybe she'd gone to one farther away, although Grace Point Chapel was within walking distance of the Maple Grove neighborhood.

After shaking hands with the pastor, he hurried down the brick steps and escaped around the corner to his rented loft over Knight's Pharmacy. Changing into something more casual, he watched the clock until it was time to drive the several miles for supper at Donovan's parents' house.

Bradley's aunt had repeatedly invited him to move into the guesthouse on the back of the property with Donovan, but he couldn't bring himself to do it. He wanted to be completely independent and successful all on his own. Parts of him were still coming together, pieces becoming new and whole…until this. Dori's best friend from college was Claire Woodbury at Henny House, and it all felt strange and familiar at the same time.

Something inside him had cracked and was urging him to find out more. Images of Dori, Claire and the fair-haired little girl spun in his mind like wheeling crows.

At the supper table, Aunt Vi questioned him on the Monroe project then, just as he'd dreaded, his cousin brought up the house.

"Bradley is going to fix up the wonky Victorian on Maple Grove Lane," Donovan declared as if it were broadcast news.

Aunt Vi straightened in surprise. "Miss Henny's house?"

Bradley forced down a lump of mashed potatoes as she turned to him with wide blue-green eyes, expecting an answer. "It's just repairs," he stammered, hoping she couldn't hear his heartbeat echoing in his ears.

"That's exciting."

"I guess," he relented, setting down his fork. "The

new homeowner isn't interested in restoring it. She wants to make modern updates."

"I'm sure you can talk her into it." Uncle Harold winked. "You talked me into letting Vi update this old place."

Bradley clasped his hands, forcing himself to be conversational and not think about Dori. His aunt's house had been one of his first projects when he'd moved to Kudzu Creek. Like Claire, she hadn't wanted to restore the old house but to update it. He'd talked her into keeping the 1980s columns and trim and focusing on the wallpaper and carpets instead.

"The Henny House needs a lot of work, but it could be a beautiful landmark for Kudzu Creek if it was preserved."

"I agree," concurred Aunt Vi with enthusiasm. "It was the finest home built in town at the turn of the twentieth century—and by a doctor who was a person of color."

"He couldn't have had it easy." Admiration filled Donovan's tone as he gave a small shake of his head. "Did you know Doctor Henny's grandson marched in the Montgomery Bus Boycott and was arrested? The NAACP here had a fundraiser to bail him out of jail."

"That would have been Miss Henny's father. She was proud of that. The Hennys have done a lot for this town," Aunt Vi reminded them. "Miss Henny was amazing to take in all of those children after she retired from teaching."

"I always did like the house," Uncle Harold admitted. "Although it looks a bit like a haunted mansion these days."

"Queen Anne originally," interjected Bradley, unable

to help himself, "then the Victorian era took over—until the eighties."

"Did I mention the historical preservation board heard about Bradley's goals and is interested?" Donovan asked.

"That's a sure way to get you on the board," remarked Aunt Vi. She dipped her chin at Bradley. "I've already spoken to Laurel Murphy, and she said your name is on the shortlist since you're an Ainsworth and all."

That news would have lifted Bradley's spirits if he hadn't known Claire had wild ideas about what do with the house. Had the historical board looked through his portfolio? Henny House's new residents and their connection to Dori loomed in his mind again. He glanced at Donovan, hinting at him to change the subject, but his cousin ignored him.

"I hear Miss Henny's heir is no spinster." Donovan smiled.

Bradley tried not to grimace.

"Is that so?" asked Aunt Vi with interest.

Donovan waved his fork in the air. "Ms. Olivia cornered me at Peachtree Market and informed me she was darling, which I think means attractive."

"Well, I'll just have to meet her," cooed Aunt Vi.

Bradley saw a gleam in her eye and felt the blood drain from his face. There would be no matchmaking here. At least not with him. Claire was one of Dori's closest friends in the last few years of her life. He cleared his throat. "Her name is Claire Woodbury."

Aunt Vi crinkled her powdered forehead. The fading corn-silk-yellow hair framing her face bounced as she shook her head. "Miss Henny had some rascals over the years."

"Claire wasn't one of them." Bradley rushed to defend Claire and wondered why. "She's very sweet, but she has a lot on her plate right now with the condition of the place. I don't think she was expecting it to be this bad."

"Why don't you be her contractor and worry about restoration talk later?" suggested Uncle Harold.

Bradley looked down at his half-eaten food. "She wants to remove the gazebo." He groaned. "It won't get me on the committee if I ruin that house with fickle trends."

"Didn't you tell me on the phone the other day she needs some wiring done? An electrical outlet?" Donovan queried.

Bradley remained silent. She *had* asked for help. He *had* offered. In fact, he'd promised her he'd come back to fix the outlet and talk about the roof. Bradley's heart prickled. He couldn't put his past behind him and build a life in Kudzu Creek with Dori's best friend living in the house he needed to restore to redeem himself. Not to mention, she had a little girl that wasn't hers, but Dori's, and people might think… He shook away the thought, but it persisted.

Little Emily. She did look like Dori, a tiny miniature, with the same fair hair and big smile, except for the dimple and dark brown eyes that looked like… Bradley's heart took a running leap and jumped into a precipice as wide and deep as the Grand Canyon. *Mine? No. Surely not.* He caught himself wavering in his seat.

"Honey, are you okay?" Aunt Vi prodded.

Bradley's lungs seemed to shrink. His lips moved but

no words came out. He squeezed his eyes shut, wondering if he would faint. Could it be the consequences of his past was toddling around Henny House?

Claire spent a few days hiding in the house like it was a fort that could protect her as Miss Henny had for so many years. She found she couldn't bring herself to unpack the rest of her things because the stinging suspicion of who the handsome contractor was had ruined her enthusiasm. Kudzu Creek no longer felt safe. It was all she could do to take Emily outside to play.

After a breakfast of oatmeal and dodging the raisins Emily kept throwing from her high chair, Claire cleaned the kitchen and followed the toddler to the back door. Emily put her hands on the screen and babbled anxiously about her trike. Sunshine arrowed through the tree branches, guiding rays of light across the small patio. Crickets whined in time to the birds' songs. With a heavy sigh, Claire muttered, "Okay, baby girl. Let's go outside and play." She couldn't stay inside the house forever. It wasn't going to change anything if her worries were true.

They tromped off the porch, and Claire pushed Emily around on the trike until she threw her head back and giggled with joy. Claire chuckled, too. It almost made her forget about their troubles.

After wearing each other out, she convinced the little girl to help her pull the weeds that had grown up against the house's foundation. Emily thought it was a game. Claire chuckled at her green hands and showed them to her. "We're going to have to get gloves from Mr. Thu!"

Emily's warbling laugh echoed across the backyard. For a split second, Claire thought she heard Miss

Henny laughing along with her. She would be so happy Claire had come home with a child. But was it to stay? Even if the house wasn't too expensive to repair, if she lost Emily, there would be no point. A pottery studio wouldn't matter. Could she live happily in Henny House without Dori's little girl?

Feeling her smile melt, Claire sat back on her heels and gazed up at the second story of the house. The gutters were heaped with leaves. Mildew splotched the faded paint behind the waterspouts. The projects required just to fix up the exterior required an army.

Claire groaned and hopped to her feet. She noticed the windows were coated with grime. At least she could wash the panes. Her hand was on the water spigot when she saw a pair of khakis come around the corner of the house. She straightened, but her heart cartwheeled into the ground.

"Hi." Bradley Ainsworth shuffled in the grass beside the patio. His eyes darted back and forth between Claire and Emily. He wore a loose salmon-colored T-shirt, and the top of his hair looked ruffled. His expression was puzzled and scared, not determined like he'd arrived to run electricity to the shed.

Claire worked her mouth but no words came out. She tried to rearrange her face into a cardplayer's bluff, sure she was failing miserably. They could pretend all they wanted, but they both clearly had questions that made this a standoff. His were written all over his face. She could almost imagine him wearing a Stetson, his hand twitching at his side. He'd look good in one, but he was holding a toolbox.

"I knocked on the front door," Bradley offered, taking another step forward. The toe of his sturdy work boot scraped across the patio. It was a strange fashion choice with his khakis. There was a shadow of a beard across his jaw again, trimmed neatly at the ear, and it made him look carefree and attractive rather than scruffy. His cheeks were red.

"Hi!" Emily broke the tension. She toddled through the grass with her arms open wide as if Bradley was an old friend she hadn't seen in a long time.

Claire's heart froze in her chest.

Bradley crouched to his knees still clutching the toolbox. "Hi, Emily," he said carefully.

Claire heard a tremor in his voice. Perspiration flowered on the palms of her hands, and she fought a whisper of light-headedness.

Emily stopped in front of the man who shared her brown eyes and lowered her arms. "Hi," she repeated rather shyly and then let out a nervous giggle. "This?" She crouched and tugged his hand off the handle of his toolbox.

"These are my tools," he whispered.

Claire watched him examine the toddler like a painting on an exhibit wall. Could it be true? How had he figured it out?

"Toy?" Emily's question was filled with wonder.

"No, my tools."

The baby fussed with the lock, but Bradley didn't help her. He just watched as she jutted her chin in concentration—something Dori always did when thinking things through. It was sweet, but Claire felt like she was going to faint.

Bradley tore his gaze from Emily and rose to his feet. He mashed his lips together so hard, they looked white. Claire felt her cheeks fill with anxious heat. Bradley's eyes looked dull and apprehensive. "I—I came to run the wiring in the shed for you."

She took a deep breath and forced herself to say something. Anything. "That's nice of you. I have some questions about the roof, too," she reminded him.

He dropped his chin, and she watched him take a deep breath of air before responding. "I don't mind. I want to do it, and to help with the rest of the house, too, but I'd like to ask you something about Emily."

Claire's knees quivered, and she wished there was a chair nearby so she could sit. She realized there was nothing to stop her from grabbing Emily and darting back inside the house, but a warm feeling fell over her shoulders like a hug from behind. What would Miss Henny do? She would be calm. She would be reasonable. And honest. Claire thought her heart would break. If Dori were here, she'd be a straight shooter, too, not that there was much choice.

"Okay." Claire felt something wet on her bottom lashes and gave a reluctant motion toward the shed.

Bradley took another deep breath as Emily pointed with frustration at the locked toolbox. He knelt beside her. "Do you want to help me carry it?"

Emily gazed at him with pursed lips then darted into the backyard to run in circles. Claire was glad it was fenced. She was thankful for the distraction, too. She felt her every nerve tingle as Bradley followed her to the shed. For some reason, it bothered her that she looked messy today with lounge pants knotted around her waist and her bangs pushed back with a headband. When she unlocked the door, she remembered with dismay that Dori and Emily's pictures were still lying on the plywood floor.

A boot thumped over the threshold as Bradley stepped inside. "Where would you like it?" His breathing sounded light and uneasy. Her gaze fell on the pictures. "The outlet," he explained, "or outlets?"

"Um, it doesn't matter." Claire swung her gaze around the room, trying to think. "I guess two would be smart."

"Here and there?" He pointed inside the door and then to the back wall.

"Yes," Claire agreed, knowing she would regret not thinking it through later. But who could think at a time like this? She'd never had a father, but if Bradley was who she thought he was then Emily had a chance, and he seemed like a very nice man. How could she deny Emily this opportunity? She should have tracked him down after the funeral. Her heart wrenched.

As if reading her mind, Bradley picked up the picture of Dori and leaned it against the wall. He set his toolbox on the floor then rested his hands on his hips. "So I guess you heard about me. You know Dori and I got together one summer. Eloped."

Tense, Claire nodded. Her spine felt as stiff as a fencepost.

Bradley crossed his arms, munched on his lip then winced. "Look, Claire," he stammered with a frown, "Dori was my childhood sweetheart, a best friend, and I loved her. I mean," he explained, "I loved her as much as any best friend or sister or cousin or whatever. We…" He hesitated, and his face reddened. "We made a mistake. It was too soon, too fast, and we didn't think it through for the long term."

"I know." Claire felt her fingers curl up. Beautiful Emily was not a mistake.

"She told you about me?"

"Yes. A little."

Bradley looked down. "We used to hang out every summer when she came to visit her grandparents at Lake Charles, and sometimes at Christmas, too." Bradley's eyes held to the plywood floor as if he were remembering something painful. "She was one of my best friends, but I guess her family had other plans for her." He looked up. "Was she happy...about Emily?"

"Happy enough," Claire assured him. "She worked part-time at a movie theater and tried to go to school."

He smiled. "She had a job?"

"She didn't need the money," Claire acknowledged, "not at first, with her parents paying for everything."

"As long as she did what they wanted," he interjected.

Claire stared in surprise. He really did know Dori. "They cut her off after they learned about the baby."

"That, I can believe." A sad smile pulled up one cheek, and she saw the crescent dimple under his cheekbone. "She was a great girl."

"She was." For a few seconds, Claire had forgotten about Emily, who was a great girl, too. A little girl. A baby girl. Without a mother or a father. Heart pounding, she watched Bradley's dark eyes.

"What about Emily?" he whispered as if hearing her thoughts.

Claire glanced out the shed window to make sure Emily was still in the yard, then forced herself to speak calmly. "Dori left her with me the night of the accident. She would have wanted me to take care of her, and so I have. I promised her the day she died."

Bradley turned his head akimbo. "What about Dori's family?"

"They don't want her." Claire could not keep the bitterness out of her voice.

Bradley sniffed as if trying to disguise a cough of contempt. "They knew about her and didn't do anything? That doesn't surprise me since it wasn't in their plans for Dori to run off and get married before becoming a doctor."

Claire found herself nodding in agreement. "They put Emily into foster care, and I was able to get guardianship."

Bradley studied Claire with something akin to gracious approval, but then his gaze returned like a lead weight to the floor. For a heartbeat, neither of them drew a breath and the silence was deafening.

"So she's mine?" he finally voiced. It came out a meek declaration that sounded more uneasy than certain.

"Yes, I believe so. I should have recognized your name." Claire's neck pinched when she made herself nod her head up and down in acknowledgment. Wanting desperately to know what would happen now, she saw Bradley's eyes swell with tears. He looked out the window and a thin drop escaped.

Claire's eyes wanted to brim over, too, but she blinked the water away. With a deep breath, she asked the question she'd had to ask too many times already in her life: "So what happens now?"

He shook his head. "I don't know." His voice wavered. "I can't tell you how much I appreciate everything you've already done. Do you have any suggestions?"

Claire remembered how she'd always gone to Miss Henny for help and the first thing her sweet momma always said in a crisis. She squared her shoulders.

"Yes. We take this one day at a time."

Chapter Four

After running a line of electricity out to the shed while listening to Emily's cheerful singing, Bradley drank the bottle of water Claire had brought to the shed before disappearing without a word. The backyard was quiet now, and he figured she'd taken the little girl indoors for lunchtime and a nap.

Hesitating on the back patio, Bradley decided to leave the situation alone a few hours so his mind would stop racing. A headache was forming at the base of his skull. The little girl had his brown eyes. His dimple. He was a dad. A *father.* The word came out of nowhere and startled him.

He thought of his frail relationship with his own parents. They'd given him everything, and he'd appreciated it by working hard and keeping their rules until he just couldn't do it anymore. What would they say when they learned he had a motherless baby? It would probably be the last straw, and they'd never speak to him again.

Bradley nearly had to gulp to breathe as he circled the house to leave. His lungs felt like they were being wrung out. He had to get away and think. He didn't want to see anyone.

"Thank you for putting in the outlets for me." Claire's soft voice broke through the deafening noise in his head. Bradley stumbled to a halt. She was standing on the front porch with a book in her hand like she'd just gotten up from one of the aluminum rocking chairs.

He shaded his eyes with a palm across his brow. The noonday temperatures were climbing. Insects buzzed. "You're welcome," he said gruffly. She held the book against her chest as if it would protect her.

"I have to get back." He excused himself, hoping she didn't suspect his desperation to escape.

"I understand. This must be a surprise."

Was she kidding? More like a tsunami.

Claire leaned against the rickety porch railing in earnest. "I'm sorry you had to find out this way. I didn't know you lived here. I was just coming back."

"I understand." Bradley's throat strangled with emotion. "I guess you didn't hear that much about me, or you would have recognized me immediately." How much did Claire know? Did she think he'd run off and abandoned Dori? Broken her heart? *It was what she wanted*, he wished he could explain, but Claire's eyes weren't accusing anymore, just sad.

"She didn't like to talk about it," Claire murmured. She looked as scared as he'd felt the moment he'd put it all together.

"I live in the loft over Knight's Pharmacy—if you ever need me."

Claire gave him a small smile that looked forced. "We're fine. I have your business card."

"That's right. Well..." Bradley hesitated, wanting

to flee. "I guess we should talk later, after I hear back from the roofers." *Much later.*

Something dimmed in her eyes like a bleak cloud had settled over them. "Okay. We'll be here."

"Right." Bradley slapped a polite smile on his face. Claire raised a hand to wave, leaning against the porch railing that separated them like a veil between two worlds. He nodded but before he could hurry away, there was a horrific sound of snapping wood. He watched in slow motion as Claire tumbled forward headfirst, and although he dropped his toolbox and leaped for the foundation of the house, he was too late to catch her. She flopped onto the hard ground with a thunk.

Without thinking, Bradley dropped beside her and pulled her into his lap. "Are you okay?"

Dazed, Claire slumped in his arms. She was warm and smelled like honeysuckle. *How could a girl smell like honeysuckle?*

"You're bleeding." Bradley dabbed at a minor scratch on her chin. It looked like it was swelling.

She cupped her hand over it and closed her eyes. "Ow," she grumbled.

An abrupt chuckle escaped from Bradley's chest. "You scared me there for a second. Does it hurt? It's not bad, just a scratch."

"I'm fine, I think." Claire took a deep breath, rubbed her hands down her arms and then wiggled her legs. "Yes, I'm okay, except for my pride." She winced then seemed to realize that he'd pulled her into his embrace. The warmth between them shot up several degrees. When she turned her head, her gaze looked as sultry as the morning mist. A poppy color stained her high cheekbones and little square chin.

"I, uh..." She gulped. She turned her flushed face away and examined the porch. "I guess I have a porch to rebuild, too."

"I'll help you," Bradley blurted.

She seemed surprised.

He shrugged. "It's what I do, and it looks like you have a lot more to fix up around here than you expected. Let me be your contractor—officially."

Claire's shoulders dropped, and he felt her relax. "Things are not going exactly as I'd imagined," she admitted in a quiet voice. A heartbeat of empathy passed between them, but then she stiffened and rose to her feet as if they had not just cuddled in the grass. She gave a dry laugh that sounded shy and brushed her fingertips across her forehead.

"Well, you were searching for a contractor, weren't you?" Bradley reminded her. "I can do a few things and gather all of the referrals for you for the rest."

"Yes, but..." Claire looked at him meaningfully, and the reality of the situation jerked Bradley out of the clouds.

What was he doing? The house was not the issue here. He had a child. A daughter. And he had no idea what to do about it. He'd always wanted a family someday, but not yet. Not now. Besides, he didn't even have a... Bradley pushed the thought of Dori away. No, he didn't have a wife, although he wanted one. He'd proved that by running off and eloping with the first girl who'd accepted him even though neither one of them had been ready. The only thing Bradley Ainsworth was good for right now was using a nail gun, and little Emily needed a home.

"I'll manage the house's repairs," he said firmly. "If

you don't want to restore what's original, I'll do it your way unless you prefer I find another contractor." He hesitated, surprised at the stubbornness he could still feel with everything hanging in the balance. "The only stipulation is you don't make me remove the gazebo," he added before he could catch himself.

The color in Claire's cheeks waned. The last thing on her mind was obviously the gazebo. "What about Emily?"

Bradley pretended to look around the yard so he didn't have to meet her eyes. "You can't do this yourself and take care of a…a baby." Bradley's lungs decided to shrink two sizes again, and he exhaled heavily so he wouldn't pass out. It was hot, and it didn't help that his life was suddenly in flames.

Claire clamped her mouth shut and stared back at him. Neither one of them had any idea what the next move was, but she needed sweat and muscle to keep a roof overhead, and that much he could give her. He just couldn't deal with Dori and the secret surprise she'd left behind right now. Claire looked like she wanted to argue but said, "I guess that'd be all right, and I have the money to pay you."

"No!" It shot from Bradley's mouth harder than he intended. "I mean you can pay my company their share, but don't worry about me. I'll work it out with them."

She drew back. "But Miss Henny left me money for updates and—"

"You'll need the money for major repairs like the roof," Bradley insisted. *Not to mention my child.* "I just…" He paused, his throat dry. "I just can't believe Dori didn't tell me about this, or you." Bradley trembled and forced himself to be honest. "I don't know what to do at the moment, but I can build a porch, or fix one anyway. Let me do that much until we sort this out."

Claire nodded mutely.

Bradley wondered how much she knew about him, his family, his friends. "Would you please…" he began then exhaled before blacking out, "not tell anyone about this? I mean," he reiterated, "about the thing."

He was making Emily sound like a virus.

Bradley squeezed the bridge of his nose. "What I'm trying to say is, could you not say anything to anyone in town about me being Emily's…" He could hardly get the word out it made him so scared.

"Father?" she finished.

Bradley opened his eyes to find Claire staring at him with a look of disappointment on her face.

"I just don't want anyone to know yet," he muttered. If word got back to his parents… He could scarcely breathe imagining their disappointment. "I need to figure things out," he said lamely.

With her lip slightly curled, Claire nodded again in agreement. She backed away a few steps and brushed at her chin that still had to be smarting. It left a tiny smear of blood. "Of course I won't tell anyone," she replied. "I have guardianship anyway." She glanced toward a window as if their little secret was staring out at them, and he saw her eyes glisten.

"I'll come back the day after tomorrow and get started on the porch," Bradley assured her. "We can talk about it then. Later." A part of him regretted arguing about the gazebo because he knew he would do anything Claire wanted if she would keep his secret quiet for now.

She bobbed her head.

He gave the old house a long, hopeful look. It had so much potential. Perhaps giving up the gazebo could be his last concession.

Of all the nerve! Claire thought. She banged a pot onto the stove as an exclamation point. Her mind was tired, and she was emotionally exhausted. She'd slipped inside and grabbed a broom after Bradley fled. The house had already been swept and the ceilings dusted, but she gave it another once-over and then, without thinking, filled a bucket and started washing walls.

Bradley had wasted no time asking the million-dollar question, but his reaction to her confirmation had not been what she'd expected. Instead of being awed he was the father of Emily Rochester, he'd paled like he felt sick. Then he set to work in the shed as if he hadn't heard the most important news of his life. Was that normal? Was that what any man would do?

Claire locked her teeth together to keep from chewing her lip. She imagined if she were a father, she would have scooped Emily into her lap and never let her go. Bradley had even tried to leave without saying goodbye!

She'd prepared herself on the front porch to ask him his intentions. Could she keep Emily? Would he take her away? It'd all been on the tip of her tongue. Claire knew what it was like not to have a mother or father. She understood what the little girl was going through. Together, they had the house and each other, but now it could all be ruined. The place was a disaster, and little Emily wasn't hers anymore.

A small sob escaped from her throat, and Claire dropped the bucket of dirty water into the kitchen sink and put her hand over her mouth. What would Dori want? Claire had tried to ask herself that every day since her friend had died. Miss Henny had given her some wonderful advice growing up—but none of it was applicable to this. Or was it? How she wished she were here.

With a tired sigh, Claire filled a copper pot so she could boil elbow noodles for macaroni and cheese. Emily loved macaroni. Claire loved macaroni. Did Bradley like it? The disappointment in his reaction rose up in her throat like bitter greens. He'd asked Claire to keep Emily a secret. She thumped the faucet off and stared into the water. What kind of person saw his little girl for the first time and wanted to pretend she didn't exist?

Claire blinked moisture from her eyes, snatched up the pot and stormed over to the stove. She peered around the corner and saw Emily had dragged her dollhouse into the hall and was shoving blocks into it. The baby was not some shameful enigma that needed to be kept hidden. Even Dori had told her parents the truth while she was carrying her. It was about five months into the ordeal, and she'd just learned the baby was a girl.

Claire smiled at the tender memory. Laughing together, they'd gone shopping for a pair of pink booties and then ice cream to celebrate. They'd both known there were only a few weeks left before Dori would quit medical school. She couldn't keep up the pace and raise a child. She wanted Emily to be healthy and safe.

Claire stirred the simmering water. Things hadn't gone as they'd hoped. The Rochesters were horrified Dori was having a baby and furious she was quitting medical school. When their daughter had refused to give up the baby or admit Bradley was the father, they'd cut off her allowance like severing a limb. Heartbroken, Dori had gone to work, and Claire had set her pottery dreams aside to put in more hours at the department store in the mall.

Her thoughts were interrupted by the slurring sound of the old doorbell.

Shoving down her irritation with Bradley and hoping he hadn't come back so soon, Claire flipped the heat on the stove off and hurried to the front door. She felt her brows raise in surprise when she saw tiny and bent Ms. Olivia holding a quivering bowl of green gelatin out like a peace offering.

"Ms. Olivia," Claire declared, "it's so good to see you." She looked over her shoulder, wondering if she should let in Miss Henny's neighbor from down the street. The house was a mess.

"I figured I'd waited long enough," Ms. Olivia said in a raspy tone. The curled brunette wig she wore over her short white hair was set back a bit too far. The gelatin shivered again. "Here," she insisted. "I remembered you loved my gelatin salad."

Claire took the antique bowl from her neighbor's hands although she'd never had the woman's gelatin and noted that it didn't look quite that appetizing. "I can't thank you enough, and I'm sorry I haven't been over yet to say hello."

"I still have the key," Ms. Olivia reminded her with a squint.

"Yes, thank you for watching the house all this time."

"You know I don't mind, dear," the neighborhood night owl assured her. "I always did it for Miss Henny when she had to leave for the day. Did you get my messages about the grass? I told Mr. Thu the grass needed cutting, but he wouldn't do it."

"Oh, yes, I know." Claire smiled. "I think he was waiting for permission. It's done now."

"Well, I gave it to him." Ms. Olivia clucked. She looked past Claire's shoulder. "I see you have a baby."

"Yes, I'm her guardian. Her name is Emily."

"Emily, eh?" Ms. Olivia rocked in her dark loafers and peered around Claire's elbow into the house. "I thought you'd be married by now."

"Oh," Claire laughed, "not me. Not yet."

"So you're just going to take in fosters like Miss Henny, huh?" The wrinkles in Ms. Olivia's face deepened, and Claire tamped down any hurt feelings. "You do remember I had to find new homes for her cats after the funeral."

"Yes, I do. Thank you. I'm sorry I couldn't come get them. It just wasn't possible."

Claire felt foolish holding the gelatin salad in the air. She pivoted a few steps to set it on a small table in the hall. "Did you get the card I sent after you locked up the house?"

"I did." Ms. Olivia had followed her inside. "I would have told you, but I didn't see you at church on Sunday."

"Ah, yes, I haven't made it to church quite yet." Claire grimaced. "I'm still unpacking and dealing with little surprises in the house."

Ms. Olivia peered into the parlor with something like approval, and Claire was glad she'd uncovered and cleaned the furniture. "Is that what the Ainsworth cousin was doing over here? I've seen him around a lot lately."

"Uh, yes, that was Bradley Ainsworth," Claire admitted. "He's going to be the contractor for the renovations I have planned." Claire realized saying this to Ms.

Olivia made it a fact. The whole neighborhood would know by tomorrow.

"He's a good boy," said Ms. Olivia. "All those Ainsworth boys are." She paused in thought and then a smile crept across her face, making her eyes brighten. "I think he's the best contractor you could ask for to fix up this place. I'm glad someone's finally doing it."

"I know, I agree," said Claire. "I'm sorry it's been an eyesore for so long. We're going to make it beautiful."

Ms. Olivia's smile widened with approval. "There now, I can't wait. And I have plenty of irises for your front yard. You can have it looking almost as good as mine next year. Miss Henny would never take them. She always said gardens were for vegetables."

Claire pushed down a laugh. "I'll definitely take you up on the offer. Anything to cut costs will help."

"Ca-re?"

Claire glanced down to find Emily at her side. She was looking up at her with beaming eyes. "I know you're hungry, baby."

"Oh, now, I don't want to take up your time. You go fix dinner for that pretty little one."

"Thank you." Claire picked up Emily and plopped her on her hip as Ms. Olivia shuffled to the front door. "Please be careful on the stairs, Ms. Olivia."

"Oh, don't you worry, Claire Henny, I haven't broken a bone in all my eighty-seven years."

Instead of reminding her she wasn't a real Henny, Claire took Ms. Olivia's elbow and helped her out anyway. "Let's keep it that way," she suggested. When the woman plodded down the sidewalk after a final wave, Claire took a deep breath and called out, "Ms. Olivia?"

"Yes, dear?"

"So you think I can trust Bradley Ainsworth to take care of things?"

"Oh, honey, I've known him since he was a boy, and his aunt and uncle and cousin all my life. You can trust him with your house."

Somewhat reassured, Claire toted Emily back into the kitchen and started the water boiling again so they could watch the macaroni noodles simmer. It was something they did when Claire cooked in the kitchen, and it felt cozy and normal, what any family would be doing this time of day. Despite the gelatin salad and inquiry, Ms. Olivia's welcome to the neighborhood had calmed something inside her. It was almost like she belonged.

She thought of Bradley. What was he doing for supper tonight? Did he eat at home? It seemed he was always coming and going from work to projects and whatever else stole his time.

His family? She cringed at the thought. Surely they were a part of his time. According to her online research, his parents still lived in Lake Charles. That was just down the road. Would he tell them about the baby?

Claire's heart squeezed with a new concern. Dori had wanted him to move on and not be held back by his family's judgment over his career path or impulsive marriage and divorce from her. If they knew he had a child, they would probably be upset. Claire frowned at the boiling water. Maybe that's why he wanted to keep things secret for now. She glanced at the green gelatin salad on the counter and sucked in an anxious breath. If Ms. Olivia figured it out before anyone else, there'd be no keeping it quiet in Kudzu Creek.

Nothing made sense no matter how long he stared at it. Bradley put the file away for the Monroe project, closed the expense report on his computer and shuffled down the hall to tell Mr. Parker good-night. It was early to be clocking out, but he was on a salary and could take work home with him. With a grumbling stomach, he tucked a stack of photos under his arm and slipped outside into the dank afternoon heat.

Southern Fried Kudzu looked like a beehive with folks buzzing in and out for afternoon treats or takeout dinners. Bradley sidestepped the outdoor tables, thinking fried food didn't sound appetizing even though he hadn't eaten all day. The Peachtree Market across the street on the corner had local produce, jams, jellies and basic groceries, but his cupboard at home wasn't totally bare. He trudged through the crosswalk, meandered over to the town memorial for veterans under the flagpole, and read the list of men and women who'd actually done something honorable with their lives. Someone tapped him on the shoulder.

"Are you thinking of joining the army?" Donovan smiled. He was in a white oxford shirt with rolled-up sleeves, his jacket looped through his arm. "Do you want an invitation to the VFW? I know people. I can get you one."

"Veterans of Foreign Wars? No," mused Bradley. He glanced up at the flag. Would there be a war between Claire and him? There didn't need to be. She was doing a fine job taking care of Emily. No need to rush in and turn everyone's life upside down. Besides, he didn't know what to do with a baby. He'd only had an older sister, and she'd started a career then married and moved to Florida, to the family's credit. He felt like he was standing on his head.

"I heard you finished the Monroe project," Donovan

confided. “She’s happy. Told my secretary she’s going to submit photos to one of the local home magazines.”

“Yes, she sent me a few to look at for my opinion.”

His cousin cocked his head. “You don’t sound excited.”

Bradley screwed up his face in an attempt to smile. “It’s been a long day.”

“New client?”

“Sort of.” His voice faltered and Donovan glanced at the Monroe project photos under Bradley’s arm. “I dropped by Henny House today and ran some electricity out to the shed,” Bradley blurted.

“So she let you. What was it for anyway?”

“She’s a potter.”

Donovan leaned forward. “What’s that?”

“A ceramist,” explained Bradley, trying to keep from unloading everything he’d just learned about Emily. “She makes pottery on one of those spinny wheels and needs a studio space for all that kind of stuff.”

“Oh, a kiln.” Donovan raised his chin in understanding. “That’s interesting.”

Bradley agreed. “I saw a couple things on her worktable. She’s talented.”

“And she’s not married.” Donovan’s eyes narrowed. “I saw her in the front yard the other day when I was cutting through to Creek Street. Pretty cute.”

Bradley licked his bottom lip. It felt dry and tired, much like him. “Yeah. I mean no. Not married.” *She just showed up with my baby.*

“What about the little girl?” Donovan didn’t bother to hide his curiosity.

“She’s not hers. She just has custody,” Bradley explained in a strangled voice.

"Grandbabies are all Mom talks about when she's not pointing out her gray hair." Donovan sighed. "So did Claire decide to hire you?"

"Yes, we worked something out." Bradley folded his arms across his chest to hide the fact his heart had started thrumming. If he was going to tell anyone…

"Are you sure you're okay?" Donovan's mouth curved down around the edges. "Did they turn you down for the historical preservation board?"

"Not yet," Bradley admitted, "but I haven't heard anything. They're not in a hurry, that's for sure."

His cousin shrugged. "They have until the end of their fiscal year. I've put in a good word for you. Don't worry."

"Thanks." Bradley turned his attention back to the memorial and rosebushes dripping with crinolines of scarlet blossoms. "Look, I may need your help in the near future," he warned. Donovan was a lawyer, after all. Bradley glanced around for anyone nearby who might overhear and lowered his voice. "It looks like I may have a…situation."

"A what?"

Bradley couldn't believe the words had come out of his mouth, either. He sucked in a nervous breath. "A father situation," he explained.

Donovan scrunched his forehead. "What's wrong with your father?"

"No." Bradley sighed in exasperation, "I mean me."

Donovan stared.

"Me, a father."

Donovan's eyes widened, and he made an *O* with his lips. He pointed. "You?"

"Yes." Bradley felt heat shoot to his cheeks like hot stars.

For the first time in his life, Donovan was speechless.

"I'm as shocked as you are," Bradley mumbled. "I just found out, so I'm going to need some time, but I'd like to know that I can call you if I need a referral or..."

"Of course you can," Donovan exclaimed, "free of charge." He rubbed his mouth with the back of his fist. "It'd be best for me to recommend someone to you, though, but wow."

"You're telling me."

Donovan lowered his voice. "Is there anything I can do right away? Who—"

Bradley gave his head a sharp shake. "I can't talk about it right now. I need to think."

"Okay, I'll pray for you then," Donovan assured him.

"That's saying a lot coming from you. Thanks."

"Don't worry, we'll work this out," his cousin said to comfort him, but the words sounded like he was in doubt and disbelief. "I just can't believe it."

"I can't either," whispered Bradley. He dropped his head back and peered at the flag then looked down the street toward the church with its lofty bell tower. Freedom and second chances? He'd moved back to Georgia for a fresh start in a new town far away from Lake Charles, his parents and his mistake with Dori. *You could have told me, Dori. You should have!* Everything he'd accomplished in San Francisco seemed meaningless now. All of the mistakes he'd thought he'd put behind him had followed him to Kudzu Creek.

Chapter Five

Claire awoke to the growling sounds of a lawnmower that faded as the sun rose higher. She wasn't sure when Bradley was going to show up and start working on the porch, but she certainly wasn't going to call to ask the handsome man.

She put a hand on her chest. It felt like a piece of her heart had been tied up in knots since the moment she'd walked into the house and caught Bradley pounding holes in the ceiling. But it couldn't be. He was Emily's father and had once loved Dori—although Dori somehow had never thought of him as more than a friend.

Claire's mind pinballed between anxiety for Emily's future and fear that they would probably be separated now. Had she been too hard on Bradley after he'd left the last time? He'd probably been in shock. She shouldn't resent him. He'd run the electricity out to the shed free of charge when he could have reacted a lot worse after she'd admitted Emily was his daughter. It was the "talk later" he'd suggested she was stressing about. Maybe that's why she'd been so upset. She'd prepared herself for a long talk, and he'd bolted.

She'd been shocked herself when Dori had told her Emily was coming into the world, and of course by now, Bradley would have moved on with his life and family. There was no use avoiding it anymore, Claire realized. He knew and, eventually, so would everyone even though she'd promised to keep it secret.

But she did need to get out a little bit more. Seeing Ms. Olivia made her realize she'd only been to the little market on Creek Street and to the power company to take care of a bill. It was time to teach Emily about the Kudzu Creek that Claire and Miss Henny loved; the little town that had given Claire the only stability she'd ever known and the courage to pursue her dreams.

Dragging the stroller off the porch, Claire prodded Emily to climb inside instead of heading for her trike. "Come on, Em," she coaxed. "Do you want to go for a walk?"

"No," Emily replied. "That." She strolled across the patio toward her trike and a pile of toy buckets and shovels.

Claire's mind raced. "How about a treat? Would you like to go get a treat?" Surely they could find a snack somewhere. The little market a few blocks away always had fresh fruit displayed on a stand outside.

Emily stopped in mid-step.

"Snacks!" Claire prodded her.

"Snacks!" Emily repeated. Convinced, Emily toddled over to the worn baby stroller and lifted a leg up like a ballerina at the barre. Claire laughed, picked her up under her arms and settled her inside. They rolled down the driveway under scattered clouds that threatened rain. The air felt clammy.

"Where are you heading?" someone called.

Claire swung her attention to Mr. Thu's yard. He was on the other side of the tropical border with a pair of pruning shears. "Just a walk." She smiled.

He lifted the brim of his straw gardening hat to see better. "I hope you don't get wet. It's supposed to shower off and on today."

"I checked my cell phone," Claire assured him, raising her phone clutched in one hand. "We have until lunchtime, I hope."

Mr. Thu grinned. "Those gadgets beat all I ever saw telling you when it's going to rain from one hour to the next."

"Weather apps come in handy," she agreed, "and you can see a live radar."

"Now that's an idea," the gardener mused. He glanced past her. "I was going to pull my edger out and trim my sidewalk real quick this morning. Do you mind if I do yours?"

Claire glanced over her shoulder at her front yard and saw the grass was short and even. "Oh my..." she began. "Did you cut my lawn again?" When she looked, his eyes widened with innocence, but his cheek twitched. "Oh, Mr. Thu. You shouldn't have. I was going to get to it. I was. It's just so hot in the afternoons, and in the mornings I have to care for Emily and then there's the house and—"

Mr. Thu held up a green gardening-gloved hand like a traffic cop. "That's what neighbors are for, or have you forgotten? Now, don't you worry about it. I didn't want to do anything before knowing the new home owner, but since we're old friends, I didn't think you'd mind letting me get some regular exercise. I don't mind at all."

Claire looked down the street at the brick homes,

some of them stately, and the long stretch of sidewalks along yards as smooth as lakes. Henny House might never fit into the neighborhood, but at least the lawn wasn't a blemish anymore. "Thank you," she said.

"Don't you worry about it." Mr. Thu lifted his chin. "I cut it for Miss Henny the last two years when it got to be too much for her. It was a part of my routine. Thank you for letting me get back to it."

Emily stood in her stroller and flapped her hand at Mr. Thu. "Hi," she called.

He grinned. "Good morning. I hope you enjoy your walk." Saluting, he darted off to get his beloved lawn tools, Claire supposed, so she sat Emily down and snapped the safety belt around her this time.

Glancing at the foreboding clouds overhead, Claire started down the sidewalk to the end of Maple Grove, eager to stretch her legs. She also wanted to see what was in the front window of the gift shop called Alabaster's she'd read about after getting Emily a snack. Would they be interested in her work?

After cruising around the far end of town, Claire's memory was refreshed. East of Maple Grove Lane was the newspaper, an antique shop, the library housed in an old schoolhouse and Pruitt's, Miss Henny's favorite ice cream parlor. After admiring a pair of snowy white capris in a boutique window, Claire crossed the street looking for the flagpole in the distance. Alabaster's was next door to the new Southern Fried Kudzu, so she pushed the stroller with determination while Emily bounced in her seat.

A few storefronts later, Claire's stomach pitched into her heart when she read the black-and-gold-foiled font across a large window: Parker and Associates Construction. The same name on Bradley's business card. The architecture and construction company looked very upscale. She wondered if he was in or if he stayed out at job sites all day.

He wouldn't be hanging out at the emerging subdivisions she'd seen sprouting up in the county on her way into town. As a historical preservationist, he'd likely be somewhere close by in his loose khakis, with keys and folders and the little wrinkle between his brows, pointing at some eave or crumbling Georgian column that just had to be saved.

Her pulse jumped two beats ahead, and she ducked her head and hurried past the office. Bradley and she hadn't run into each other in town yet, but she wasn't sure either one of them was ready for that. They really needed to talk, she knew, but not out and about. At Henny House where it was safe.

Alabaster's. It was the same pink-brown brick as the rest of town, but it also featured a lovely pinstriped sunshade stretching from window to window. Centered between them was an antique door painted pearl with a lovely eucalyptus wreath. Hesitant to go inside such an elegant shop with so many breakable things while she had Emily in tow, Claire browsed the displays arranged artfully in the windows. There were embroidered towels and aprons, a slew of beautiful bracelets and rings by a local jeweler, a regional authors' book display and a cake stand heaped with handmade soaps and lotions.

Squinting to see inside the shop, Claire could make out a lineup of ceramic mugs that probably had charming expressions hand-painted on them. There were no other handmade dishes. Her heart flowered with hope. She thought of her favorite olive oil cruet on the kitchen counter at home. Perhaps she could bring it by as a sample. Cruets and pitchers were her favorite pieces to make.

Emily slumped in her seat and groaned. Tired of waving at strangers and pointing at dogs, she threw her head back. "Snacks!" she reminded Claire.

Claire patted Emily's locks and tapped her little chin. "Okay, sweetheart. Let's find snacks."

Green table umbrellas fluffed in the stiff breeze as the sun peeked through the cloud cover long enough to spotlight the street. Southern Fried Kudzu had its glass door braced open with a painted brick. Two customers darted out, gripping takeout bags like they held something sacred in them. Claire's eyes widened as a mouthwatering fragrance wafted through the humid air.

"Snacks," sang Emily in a mesmerized voice.

In full agreement, Claire guided the stroller between the outdoor seats and over the threshold into the eatery. Claire's mouth watered. Why she'd waited so long to check out the renovated coffee shop, she didn't know.

As Emily wiggled in her seat with excitement, Claire pasted a smile on her lips. A chalkboard menu over the steel countertop promised a culinary adventure from baked cheese grits and biscuits to chicken salad and other brunch delights. She passed a pair of ladies carrying trays to an open table. One of them turned her head to stare, and Claire looked down, feeling self-conscious. Perhaps they were wondering if she was new in town or just passing through.

"Can I help you?" A young woman with sleek dark hair past her shoulders leaned forward from behind the counter. A lopsided tag pinned over her heart read McKenzie.

Claire scanned the board. "I'm not sure. I mean, I know I don't want fried kudzu. Is that for real?"

"It's actually not that bad if you like greens." McKenzie chuckled.

Emily reared up, jerking at her safety belt. "Snack," she called with the authority of a two-year-old who understood how eating out worked.

McKenzie peeked over the counter. "Aren't you adorable? What would you like, honey?" She glanced back up at Claire.

"I think we just wanted something light. Sweet is okay."

The server motioned toward a narrow display case. "We have pastries and cookies if you don't want a biscuit or sandwich of the day."

Claire glanced at the menu again. The soup of the day was gazpacho—a cold tomato soup. The chicken salad sandwich was the lunch deal. She turned to the glass case. "I think we'll just have two of those fruit tarts."

"Strawberry-blackberry?"

"Yes," Claire decided. "That sounds delicious, McKenzie."

McKenzie introduced herself as "Mac," gave Claire the total and hurried over to the case, pulling plastic gloves over her hands. Feeling eyes on her, Claire glanced back at the two older women seated nearby. They were waving at Emily. One of them gave Claire a wide smile. She forced herself to smile back and released a nervous breath as she turned around. Everyone knew Miss Henny. Even if they didn't remember Claire from high school, they would know the Henny House.

"Here you go!" Mac leaned over the counter and

dropped a white paper bag into Emily's hands. The toddler squealed with excitement, and both women laughed. After thanking her and wheeling Emily over to a table, Claire was almost seated when the lady with silver-streaked, shoulder-length hair called out.

"Excuse me?"

"Yes?" Claire wheeled around, wondering if her table was reserved.

"Hi." The woman stood and crossed the distance between them. "We were just admiring your baby and wondered if you would like to sit over here with us."

Claire hesitated. Emily wasn't exactly her baby. "Adult company?" the lady teased. "I'm Viola. You can call me Vi."

The woman's friend stood and pushed out a fourth chair to make room for the stroller. She was petite, pear-shaped and wore rimless glasses. Her platinum locks were as short as Claire's. "We insist," she announced, "and I'm Diane."

"Thanks." Claire breathed a sigh of relief. Emily ripped the bag down one corner. She grabbed an entire pastry upside down, and the fruit smashed against her palm. "I wouldn't mind a little adult company this morning."

They chuckled, and Vi helped Claire wrangle the takeout bag from Emily's steely grip while her friend, Diane, wiped the baby's hands down as best she could with a paper napkin. The little girl went right back to smashing the fruit tart into her mouth.

Claire sighed and sat back. She introduced herself, explained she had moved into Henny House and how she had known Miss Henny while nibbling on her treat. Her new friends sipped tea over chicken salad and shared their memories of Miss Henny and all of the good she'd done in Kudzu Creek.

"For so many," said Diane with an awed shake of her head. "She would join any committee at church that was short-staffed, no matter if it was funeral food or janitorial work."

"I remember." Claire smiled. "She was like that. Everyone's needs came before her own. I wouldn't have made it through high school if it weren't for her."

"So you're the one at Henny House," said Vi in a mysterious tone.

"How long were you here before?" quizzed Diane.

Claire explained how she'd moved in with Miss Henny at the end of seventh grade and stayed until she'd left for Birmingham to go to college. She didn't recognize the name of Vi or Diane's grown children, but she'd kept to herself in high school. Miss Henny was her friend, and that was all she'd needed until she met Dori in the college dorms. Neither of the women at the table pried into her childhood nor mentioned foster care. For that, Claire liked them even more.

"So where do you plan to sell your pottery?" asked Diane with an arched brow after Claire told them about her work. "I happen to own the boutique next door."

"Alabaster's?" Claire suddenly felt as light as a feather. "I was hoping to put some things on consignment in your store." She opened her mouth to describe her bowls, pitchers and oil cruets when Vi turned her head. Feeling someone behind her, Claire glanced back with an eerie sensation burning between her shoulders. Her stomach flip-flopped when she saw it was Bradley.

He looked handsome in a pair of blue khakis and a bright green golf shirt, but if his eyes could have shot lasers, they would have been blasting through her. His face looked pale like he'd stood too fast, but something flickered under his cheekbone while he worked his jaw.

"Bradley, hi," she spluttered, aware the other two women had stopped speaking.

"Claire," he replied in a tight voice "Nice to see you here." There was a question in his tone, and Claire noticed he didn't drop his gaze even an inch to acknowledge Emily.

"Um, um, um!" Emily bounced in her seat, making satisfied noises while mashing her jaws together.

"I brought Emily in for a snack," Claire said carefully. Heat brushed over the apples of her cheeks. Why was he making it weird? Tense? Did he expect her to never leave the house now that they knew one another?

"We were just talking to Claire about her art," interjected Vi. She scooted back in her chair and gave Bradley the once-over. "Are you all right, honey? On an early lunch break?"

Claire swung her attention back to Bradley in consternation. Sensing her confusion, Vi chuckled. "I'm Bradley's aunt," she explained.

"Oh, I see," offered Claire after a painful pause. She understood Bradley's discomfort now. If he wasn't ready to tell his family, she needed to respect that, but he didn't have to look so horrified.

"I was just getting something to eat," he faltered. Locking his jaw, he strode away.

Claire watched him beeline to the counter. Taking a deep breath, she turned back to the table with what she hoped was a bright smile. Diane's eyes were round with curiosity. "Bradley's helping me with some work around the house," Claire explained.

"That's right," Vi recalled. "He was hoping to buy it, but he told us he's going to work with you on restoring it instead."

"Repair." Claire differed; she had no intention of restoring everything back to its original condition. Bradley knew that. She'd made it clear. Henny House was going to have the beautiful ceramic floor tiles and modern kitchen and baths she'd always dreamed about.

"I always loved that wraparound porch," Diane admitted with a wistful gaze. "I'm glad you're fixing up the place."

Miss Henny had spent every afternoon on that porch waiting for Claire to come home. Before she could share that, Emily tried to stand, jerking on her safety belt again. She held up her arms to be picked up. "Out!" she demanded.

Claire glanced toward Bradley at the counter. "Miss Henny always meant to do the updates, but she stayed so busy with other things, it slipped her mind."

"Oh, I understand," sighed Vi. "Bradley just helped us renovate our home last year when he moved to town. It was his first project here, and quite a challenge because we hadn't done anything to it since we bought it thirty-five years ago. Luckily, he had plenty of time."

"Out!" Emily pleaded again.

Diane wadded up her napkin, a signal she would be hurrying off soon.

"I should go," Claire announced. Bradley stood a few feet back from the counter now with his arms crossed over his chest, and she decided she didn't want to be forced into another stilted conversation with him. She thanked his Aunt Vi for the table invitation, promised

Diane she'd come visit about the pottery then pushed Emily and all of her sticky mess out the front door.

Rather than continue down the street to the little park around the flagpole, Claire veered right to return to the neighborhood. She suspected Bradley had no desire to converse with her or Emily at Kudzu's, and it stung a little bit. A lotta bit actually. True, it was a painful situation and awkward, but the sooner they both dealt with it, the better. Even if that meant—

Wait. Panic rippled through her chest. What was she thinking? If Bradley told everyone Emily was his, other people would get involved. Even if he didn't usurp custody from her—which he had every right to—his family might. After all, Vi had found Emily endearing and enjoyed her antics.

The tart in Claire's stomach formed a wad that felt like glue, and nausea pushed its way up her throat. How had Miss Henny let go of the children she'd fostered and loved? Claire clenched her teeth and quickened her pace to get home as fast as she could until it strained the muscles in her calves. "We should have never walked into town," she wheezed, but Emily wasn't listening. She'd leaned back against her seat and hung her feet over the front of the stroller to take it easy.

Along the sidewalk, Claire saw the grass had been neatly edged in front of Henny House. Mr. Thu had come through as promised. She was almost to the driveway when she heard steady footsteps behind her.

"Claire."

Bradley's voice sent shivers down her spine and for all the wrong reasons. She wanted to see him again. She wanted to talk. But not like this. And not about the mountain between them. Claire took a deep breath as a gust of wind billowed across the sidewalk announcing rain. A deep-throated growl rumbled across the skipping clouds overhead.

"Uh-oh!" Emily rattled the sides of the stroller and announced her concern.

"I thought you were eating your lunch." Claire slowed to a stop.

"I had it sent over to the office," Bradley explained in a hoarse tone. His eyes looked darker than usual, an onyx shade of brown as deep as a hollowed-out log. He stopped a foot away. "What were you doing at Kudzu's?"

"I told you. We were having a snack."

"With my aunt?"

"I didn't know she was your aunt. She said her name was Vi when she introduced herself and asked me to sit with them."

Bradley let out a small breath. "I just—"

Claire tried not to frown. "Emily has a right to go anywhere I take her."

"I know." Bradley ran his fingers through his hair, and Emily straightened in her stroller, craning to look up at the familiar man beside her. "Hi," she whispered shyly and gave him the sweetest smile. He lowered himself to her level, folded his arms over the tops of his knees, and stared. Emily met his gaze a few seconds then pointed at the rainbow on her yellow cotton T-shirt. "Pony."

Bradley's face softened. He offered a finger, and she squeezed it. A soft chuckle worked its way out, but he quickly sucked it back in with a quiet gasp. "This is… I mean Dori left and—"

Claire's heart sank. She saw now that Dori might not have made the best decision after all. Just because she hadn't wanted to be a part of Bradley's life or upset his family didn't mean it had been right to keep Emily a secret. Claire could have still kept Emily, and Bradley wouldn't have been blindsided when he'd stepped into Henny House.

Kudzu Creek. It was a strange name, but she didn't want to leave this place. It was the happiest time of her life, and Miss Henny was as close to having something permanent and real as she'd ever had. "Dori might have left," Claire choked out, "but Emily can't do that. She has nowhere to go, and no one." Her throat tightened. "Except for me—and this house."

"Dori should have told me," Bradley insisted in a wounded voice. He unfurled and stood beside the stroller, studying Claire. A fat raindrop pelted the top of her head.

Claire always knew she would have to find him and tell him everything someday. That was another reason she'd moved back to Georgia—she knew Emily's father was from the area. Just not this close. She looked at the house and its protective front porch with the round gazebo large enough for parties.

"I never knew my parents, so I wouldn't have denied Emily her chance in the long run."

Bradley gazed at her pensively. "Maybe, but either way, I'm going to need your help figuring this out." His voice crackled with injury.

Raindrops began to spatter around them on the concrete like the clouds were shaking out soaked towels. Emily shrieked in delight. Claire ducked her head and reached for Bradley's arm. It was solid and warm, and she wanted to hang on to it for as long as possible because it felt nice. More than nice. She cupped her hand over her eyes and looked at the sky. Down the street, she saw Ms. Olivia standing under an umbrella at her mailbox. Claire waved. "We better get inside." She sucked in a breath of courage. "I think you should come in with us, too."

The kitchen looked tidy and smelled like pine-scented cleaner. Wallpaper had been peeled down to the drywall. A shapely and well-used oil cruet rested on the old countertop; a beautiful blue bowl held lemons on the dining table. As Claire carried Emily off for a nap, Bradley sank into the recovered banquette and slid his hand over the new fabric wondering if she'd done it herself.

"I found the fabric online," Claire informed him as she walked in.

"It's nice." Bradley's mind hopscotched between Emily, Dori, and Claire and the changes taking place inside Henny House.

"It's stain-resistant." Claire pulled out a chair across from him and swiped her slanted bangs behind her ear.

Bradley locked gazes with her. Her eyes were as soft as the lake on an overcast morning. More silver than gloomy. Her jaw looked like she was pressing her back teeth together.

After a long silence, with only the sound of the pouring rain outside filling the air around them, Claire put her hands on the table and gripped one thumb over another like she needed to hold on to something. "What do you want to know about me and Emily?" she asked in a quiet voice. "I owe you that much."

Bradley cleared his throat to give himself time. The bowl of lemons sat between them like neutral territory, and he picked one up to study it while trying to organize his whirling thoughts. When thunder rumbled outside the window, they both jumped. "So, you were her college roommate. I'm sorry I didn't remember your name. She talked about you sometimes."

"That's okay," Claire whispered.

"I did love Dori..." he began. "I wanted to make it work. She was the oldest friend I had, and I believed it'd become more special over time. You know, more..." Bradley straightened in the seat, his nearly-forgotten feelings of betrayal bubbling to the surface. "So what now? How long have you had Emily?"

"Since Dori died. I mean—" Claire tucked the hair behind her ear again "—I kept her after the accident until Dori's parents got involved and put her into foster care, but I couldn't bear it." She sniffed and looked away. "I found out how to get her back and did what it took. Her grandparents signed over custody."

Bradley's eyes narrowed. "What about mine? My parents?"

Claire winced, and her cheeks flowered with color. "I'm sorry to tell you this, but your name isn't on the birth certificate."

A soft gasp shot from Bradley's mouth. Claire raised a small shoulder in a defensive shrug. "Don't think of it that way. Dori didn't want to do something like that until she had your approval."

Bradley wilted into the seat. "It's hard to believe she only did that because she cared." Bitterness worked its way up to his tongue.

"If you knew her like I did, and I know you did, then you must believe it," insisted Claire.

"You said you were going to—"

"Yes," Claire blurted. "I knew I would have to do it someday, but I thought you were in California, and I… I love Emily." Her voice cracked. "I wasn't sure you'd even want to know. My birth father never did. So I thought I'd put it off and keep a part of Dori to myself for a while until the time felt right."

Bradley ran his fingertip over the lemon's rind and resisted the urge to squeeze it. "I guess I should thank you then." He heard the faint sarcasm in his tone. "No, I'm sorry. I should thank you. If it wasn't for you, Emily would have been raised by complete strangers. I might have never known."

The enormity of the situation turned into soul-gutting gratitude in Bradley's heart. He lifted his gaze and found Claire studying him. "I'm not sure what to do next other than take a blood test and find out how to change her birth certificate, but can you…" How did one ask a stranger to keep a child under her roof? He glanced up. A spot of water was pooling on the most stained ceiling tile.

Claire followed his gaze. "I can still keep her for the time being—I want to—and for as long as you'd like even when we transfer things over," she offered. He heard unspoken pleading in her tone.

A swollen teardrop formed overhead. They both watched it fall and splat on the worn floorboards. "Will you help me with my roof?" she asked.

A smile tugged at the corner of Bradley's mouth, and he relented. "I was going to start on the porch tomorrow and get a referral about the roof for you anyway. How about we climb into the attic and find out where this water is coming from for right now?"

Chapter Six

A week after setting a date with Diane to bring her ceramics to Alabaster's for consignment consideration, Claire gathered her things, thankful Bradley was both comfortable and excited to babysit Emily for a short time on his lunch break.

"Remember, she lies down right after she has her snack," Claire reminded him. She was wrapping her best cruet and the kitchen table's blue fruit bowl with turquoise-colored tissue.

"We know," chanted Bradley, bouncing a grass-stained Emily on his hip. She pointed at the fridge and he opened it to pull out her sippy cup.

"Make her use words," Claire admonished him. She folded the flaps of the box over its top. Bradley bounced Emily again as she tried to drink, and she spurted the chocolate milk he'd bought her down her chin in laughter. "Oh!" Claire sighed, but Bradley used his shirt-sleeve to wipe off the toddler's mouth before Claire could grab a towel.

"Don't worry, Ca-re, we know the routine. I'll finish up the last coat of paint on the porch when you get back and see about picking up the nails in the yard the roofers left behind."

Claire glanced overhead and noted the patched ceiling tiles. "I'm glad all that noise is over. Thanks for taking care of it so I can pull this ceiling down and install new drywall."

He cringed. "That's very modern, but you could cover it with rescued antique tin ceiling tiles. They'd look nice painted off-white."

"The walls are Sea Glass Gray now. It needs to be bright white."

Bradley looked around at the freshly painted walls she'd finished and shrugged. "A vintage crimson color would have been nice."

"Too dark," she countered, "and old-fashioned."

"What color did Miss Henny have before the ivy wallpaper?"

"Mustard," quipped Claire, "which is why she decided to wallpaper."

"Snack," Emily reminded them.

"Cheese puffs," agreed her father.

Claire shook her head in surrender and picked up the box of packed pottery. "How about carrots, hummus and grapes? They're in a plastic baggie on the top shelf." She motioned with her chin toward the refrigerator.

"Aw," grumbled Bradley, "a few cheese puffs would go perfect with that."

Claire juggled the box in her arms and grinned at his mischief. "Just make sure she gets a nap, or she'll be a monster this afternoon."

"Don't worry, and good luck at Alabaster's. Diane is a sweet lady and very supportive of local artisans."

Claire shot him a wince. "Let's hope she likes my

pottery, and maybe the Peachtree Market will, too. These are the best pieces I have, but there are more in storage. I just haven't had time to get serious in the shed since I moved in the air conditioner unit and my equipment."

"Shed? You mean the studio. And she'll love them. I bet they go fast." Bradley pulled Emily's high chair away from the wall and pushed it up to the table. "You better head over there before Diane closes up for lunch. Don't worry about us. I can handle things."

He winked at her, and Claire's heart sashayed. Tingles and heart tremors every time she thought of Bradley were becoming a daily occurrence even if he was covered in dirt, sawdust or paint. Accepting his offer to help her with the house's repairs had been a good decision, but spending almost every day with him was becoming too comfortable. It'd help if he weren't so kind and cheerful, not to mention tireless and talented with his hands. She squeezed her eyes shut in a long blink and made herself quit thinking about his hands, and then his arms, and what it'd feel like to be wrapped up in them.

"Be a good girl, Emily," Claire called as she swept out of the room. She tried to push away the worries about her growing responses to Bradley as she backed down the driveway. It was challenging. She liked to watch him while he worked. Sometimes she'd hand him things and their fingers would brush together, and she'd have to look away to keep him from seeing her reaction. Once she had even caught herself looking for a sign of where he'd worn a wedding band. *Why*? She'd scolded herself. Her plate was full. There was no time for romantic interests, not with a little girl to care for and a dilapidated old house to turn into a home. Really, she wasn't any different than Miss Henny, and besides, Bradley was clearly only interested in the house and his little girl.

Turning the corner, Claire clattered the car over Creek Street's cobblestones until she saw a parking space between Diane's shop and Southern Fried Kudzu. Alabaster's was certainly within walking distance from Henny House, but because it was hot outside, and she hadn't wanted to juggle an awkward box the entire way, she'd let Bradley talk her into driving the couple of blocks.

How Dori could have only found him cute was a mystery. He was achingly handsome, and his soft voice and good humor made it impossible not to be hypnotized by him. To Emily's delight, and to Claire's, too, if she was honest, he came over every morning, and after he worked on the house, he played with Emily until she took her nap.

The only serious tension between Claire and him anymore was the mild arguments on what kinds of changes to make. She wanted the modern improvements, but the stubborn renovator still pushed her with suggestions to rescue, repair and restore. There was something magical, he insisted, about taking something broken and making it new again instead of replacing it. As an artist, Claire understood, but sometimes she wondered if he was talking about himself.

A sign on the door of Alabaster's read *Open*. Claire took a moment after parking the car to exhale a tight breath she'd been holding. She sniffed in frustration at her aching heart and wandering mind. She had more important things, like successful sales, to worry about.

Giving Diane her best pieces now would pay off later. Wetting her lips, Claire checked her hair in the rearview mirror then climbed out of the car to retrieve her box of ceramics. She found Diane at a walnut-stained counter covered with mini displays of magnets and moisturizers and floral coin purses.

"It smells wonderful in here." Claire inhaled deeply with pleasure as she approached the counter. Country music whispered from hidden speakers in the corners. A few ceiling fans stirred the air. Lace, earrings, candles and dish towels were everywhere.

"It's from scented plug-ins," revealed Diane. "I used to light candles, but the kids would stick their fingers in them, and I had to worry about fires."

"Oh. Ow." Claire laughed. She held up the moving box. "I brought you some things to look at like we talked about."

"Wonderful. I'm glad you called me back." Diane pulled the box over to her side of the counter and opened it.

Claire scanned the room behind her, feeling like she was about to be graded on a school project. "Do you mind if I wander around?"

"Of course not." Diane pulled out the cruet and unwrapped it carefully. "Oh, this is nice." She looked inside. "Never used," Claire assured her. "I keep it on my kitchen counter just for looks."

The store owner turned it in her hands. "It's really good, and a perfect fit. I sell flavored olive oils, you know."

"Do you?" Claire's tone mirrored the wonder she felt as she looked around the room and saw a white-painted cupboard across the store. There were green glass bottles of oils lined up in neat rows. The bell on the front door jangled as another customer came in, and Claire took the opportunity to investigate the oils. She heard Diane ask about a meeting at the chamber of commerce.

Blood Orange. Tuscan. Garlic and Onion… Claire studied the olive oil flavors and tried not to eavesdrop.

"—Ainsworth working on the Henny House." The familiar words pierced her ears, and Claire looked over her shoulder.

A tall woman with enormous diamond earrings and snow-white coiffed hair stood before the counter in heels. The back of her slacks had perfectly straight seams. Diane caught Claire's eye for a moment then returned her attention to her customer. "Well, you're in the right place at the right time, Laurel. Claire Woodbury lives in Henny House, and we're going to sell her pottery here."

The woman, Laurel, turned on a sharp heel and watched Claire approach. Her eyes swelled behind her tortoiseshell-framed eyeglasses, then she darted her gaze around the shop before returning to Claire. "You're Miss Henny's…relative?"

Claire didn't blink. "Not exactly," she replied. "She was my foster mother, and I lived with her for a number of years."

"Well," crooned Laurel, making no attempt to hide her curiosity, "I assumed it would be real family, having such a special history and all."

Claire's teeth almost clacked together when she closed her mouth to keep from a retort. Sensing a misstep, Diane held up the cruet. "I love these, Claire, the cruet and the bowl. They'll sell fast in the front window if I don't take them home myself."

Despite the frosty feeling in the air, Claire found herself smiling. "That would be wonderful, Diane. I should be able to bring in three to four new pieces a month if you're interested."

"I certainly am." Diane beamed. She held up the glazed blue ombré fruit bowl and let the light bounce off the surface. "This won't last long," she predicted.

"I keep lemons in it. The contrast of the colors is beautiful."

"It is stunning." Laurel wrenched her mouth to one side and held out a hand for the bowl. "And you made this?"

"I did," said Claire, straightening with pride. She could tell the woman was impressed even if she wouldn't say so.

"So I understand you hired Bradley Ainsworth to restore Miss Henny's shabby old place," Laurel queried instead.

Claire rested an elbow on the counter. Hired? It wasn't exactly how it'd happened, but she wasn't about to explain the details to this woman. "He's helping me with some things on the house, yes," she agreed. "I'm updating it, actually, not restoring very much, although he has talked me into keeping some of the floors and a few walls of beadboard."

Laurel's head tilted to one side and she dropped her sleek brows so low they touched her upper lashes. "I know the roof was replaced. We could hear the hammering all over town. You are going to keep the gazebo, aren't you?" she demanded. "They held chamber of commerce meetings in the summers there way back when. My grandmother was the president for years."

"Oh, is that so?" Claire remarked, trying to sound

impressed. "I think I remember Miss Henny mentioned that. She was a member, too."

"Yes," Laurel continued, "I suppose she was. Kudzu Creek is a small town but a historic one. Most of us have ancestors who lived here from the beginning. I do. That's why I serve on the historical preservation board as well as attend chamber meetings."

"That's admirable," admitted Claire. "I'm not from here originally. I've lived all over Georgia and spent a few years in Birmingham."

"In historical homes?"

"Well, not exactly," began Claire, stifling a chuckle.

"But you will keep the gazebo and front porch on Henny House."

Laurel's inquiry sounded more like an instruction. Claire took a breath. "As far as right now, the porch is getting repaired and painted, but I want to tear the gazebo down so the porch looks the same on both sides. I won't use it anyway. It's just me."

Laurel looked aghast. Diane smiled. "It'll look nice without it, too."

"It most certainly will not," Laurel retorted. "The gazebo is original. Dr. Henny added it for his wife in 1902. I would think Mr. Ainsworth would have explained that to you."

"Yes, he did," confessed Claire, secretly pleased Diane thought it was a good idea, "but it makes the house look so old-fashioned to me. If he won't do it, I'll have to hire someone else."

"If you wanted a newer house, you could have moved into one of the subdivisions outside of town," sniffed Laurel.

Claire tried not to cringe. "Miss Henny left me this

house, and I know she'd want me to do whatever I wanted to it. She always encouraged me to be creative. She's the one who inspired me to continue taking pottery classes after high school and to major in art."

"You're an art major?" Laurel intoned, as if the pottery she'd just admired looked like it'd been done by a kindergartner.

"I am."

"It sure shows," interjected Diane. She pried the bowl out of Laurel's hands and told her what she planned to sell it for. The woman's mouth dropped as Claire's heart rose with gratitude. "You're very talented," Diane assured Claire. "We have an Art Walk two Saturdays a year in Kudzu Creek, and the next one's coming up. I'd like to sponsor you. We'll pay for your booth, too."

Ripples of joy made Claire feel like she could cry. "I can't thank you enough for that, Diane."

"Yes," expounded Laurel, "the Art Walk was my idea a few years ago." She put a thin wrist on her hip, jangling several thin gold bracelets. "Tourists drive through on occasion and stay in our bed-and-breakfasts. *They* are historically preserved. The Art Walk is a big weekend draw."

"I'll put it on my calendar," Claire promised. She said nothing more about her plans for Henny House. They wouldn't change her mind. She backed away to escape, but before she could say goodbye, Laurel asked, "How long do you plan on living in Kudzu Creek, Claire? I always thought someday Henny House could be a charming bed-and-breakfast if it was restored properly."

"Laurel's the chairperson of the historic preservation board," Diane supplied.

"I see," offered Claire as it all came together. Laurel

Murphy might as well be mayor, too, it appeared. "As far as I know, I intend to stay in Kudzu Creek for good, and a bed-and-breakfast is not in my plans."

After a pause, Laurel said, "What a shame," and Claire waved goodbye and sped out the door.

Bradley signed the last of the paperwork for his boss and escaped next door to Kudzu's with an exhale of relief. Donovan had texted about meeting for lunch since he was in between court appointments and didn't like eating in his office.

"Where's the fire?" Bradley teased as he dropped his phone and sunglasses onto a table.

Donovan looked up from thumbing through a document. "I've eaten cold chicken and leftover green bean casserole for three days in a row with Judge Sheldon," grumbled his cousin.

Bradley snorted. "He's generous to share his packed lunches with you. What's he always say? 'Waste not, want not'?"

Donovan sighed and scrambled out of his seat to follow Bradley to the register. Mac was at the counter packing to-go orders into plastic bags. "Sorry, we're a little behind," she confessed.

"It's not a problem. Did Barney not show up?" Bradley craned his head over the register to look for the head cook who made the best Reuben sandwiches in the county.

"No, he's here," said Mac. "We just have a lot of orders today and fell behind this morning because of an unexpected visitor."

"The health department?" Donovan sympathized.

She jumped when the phone next to her jangled. "No,

thank goodness, because that would've been awkward. We had a clever little mouse-hunter sneak in through the back door at some point yesterday, and he helped himself to the coffee creamer during the night."

"A cat?" guessed Bradley, and Donovan laughed. Mac nodded. "I'm not surprised." Bradley chuckled. "What'd you do with him?" He hoped they hadn't sent the poor thing back into the streets.

"Why?" Mac wondered with sudden interest. "Would you like a kitten?" Her gaze flitted hopefully between Bradley and Donovan.

Donovan held up his hands. "We have two dogs and three cats and a partridge in a pear tree at our house. My mother doesn't need another pet."

Mac shifted her attention to Bradley. "Would you like a free kitten? He's thin and all alone and super sweet. I'll make your chocolate milk on the house."

Bradley ran through a mental list of excuses why he couldn't take custody of a cat. "I'll have to think about that," he hedged. "How did you know I was going to order chocolate milk?"

Mac lifted her brows. "You always order chocolate milk, rain or shine."

With a chuckle, Bradley backed up to scan the menu, although it was the same and he knew it by heart. It was something to do while he came up with a solid reason he couldn't take the kitten.

A sudden commotion in the back kitchen sent pots and pans flying, and Bradley heard Barney shout. Mac spun about just as a blur of gray shot around the corner and raced past the counter. Customers' heads turned as the animal jumped up on the table closest to the exit and rested its paws on the window. Everyone awwed and laughed.

"Oh, no!" Mac cried in exasperation. "I had him cornered in the office!" Barney burst from the grill with a broom, Mac hurdled over an empty chair and three different customers jumped up to chase the kitten down.

Bradley watched the circus with amusement until Diane from Alabaster's scooped it up with her free hand while holding a hot coffee in the other, and passed it to Mac like it was no big deal. The server pressed the animal to her chest and hurried to the counter. "I'll be right back," she promised Bradley and Donovan. The kitten was a powder puff of slate gray and white fur. Big round eyes, curious and entertained, peered out from between two giant pointed ears.

"He looks like a bat," Bradley declared.

"Call animal control," Donovan suggested.

"No!" Bradley blurted.

His cousin looked at him with surprise. Mac stopped in her tracks and stared.

"Don't get rid of it," he stammered. "You said it was clever and smart."

"He is." Mac held her breath.

A strange ripple of energy skipped down Bradley's back. No mother. No caretaker. Clever and sweet and all alone. He knew what Claire would do if she were here. "Okay." He jutted his hands out. "I'll take it."

Beside him, Donovan's mouth fell open. Mac smiled ear to ear. "You are so kind, Bradley Ainsworth."

"It is a nice thing to do, but you rent a loft over the pharmacy that doesn't allow pets," Donovan reminded him.

Too late. The furball was handed over. Bradley tried

to hold the kitten under the front legs, but it squirmed in alarm.

"No, hold him against you," Mac chided him.

"Oh," Bradley grunted, dodging needle-sharp claws, "like a baby."

"That's right." Mac beamed. The phone rang again like a ship's bell. "I'm sorry," she said, smoothing down her shirt. "I need to get that, and I'll be right back with you gentlemen."

Bradley held the kitten against his chest. It calmed, and he could feel a rapid heartbeat against his breastbone.

Donovan reached over and scratched it behind the ears. "Like a baby? Since when do you know how to hold a baby?"

Bradley pasted a pretend smile across his face. Donovan quirked his brow. "Wait. Does this have something to do with our little talk last month about you needing a lawyer?"

"I'm going to need some advice," Bradley admitted.

Donovan looked worried. "About what?" he pressed in a careful tone. "You haven't seemed ready to talk about it, so I haven't asked."

"How to change a birth certificate."

His cousin flinched. "You're sure then. Maybe we should talk about this in my office," he murmured, looking around. Bradley gave a quick nod. "What about that?" Donovan pointed at the little cat. "What are you going to do with it?"

Bradley ran his fingers through the kitten's soft down so different than the rough materials he worked with every day. It radiated a warmth that felt like innocence and love. It was just like holding Emily. "I've never had a pet," he admitted, "not even growing up. It was always about me."

"Well, a cat will give you a run for your money."

"I can't have it in the loft since pets aren't allowed, so I guess I'll give it to Emily." Bradley realized he'd made the decision the moment he'd seen the kitten pawing at the front window to get out.

"What about Claire?" questioned Donovan. "And by the way, I'm not ignorant of the fact you spend more time at her house than you do the office, project notwithstanding."

"She won't mind." Bradley was guessing. "I can't imagine her turning away a..."

"Stray?"

"Yes," Bradley agreed in a soft tone.

The kitten looked up at him with adoring eyes and he realized everything that Claire had gone through as a foster kid must have counted for something. It'd made her who she was. Gentle and caring. Patient and loving. Strong, too. She lived with purpose.

What was his? Was the most important thing in the world restoring houses for glory and prestige? Would his life end if he didn't get on the historical preservation board and impress his parents with his success? No. None of it ultimately mattered. All that mattered was that he had a daughter.

"Are you sure there's not something more going on over there other than stripping wood floors and fostering a kid?" Donovan wasn't teasing now. He waited pensively for Bradley to reply.

Giving the kitten a little bounce in his arms, Bradley sent his cousin a steady stare. "You didn't know this, but Claire was best friends with Dori. That's why I need to talk to you about birth certificates and the little girl at Henny House."

After an amazed pause, Donovan whispered, "Oh… wow. The little girl? She's… That's why you needed advice."

Bradley nodded. "Yes. She's mine. I might never had known if I hadn't tried to buy Henny House."

"Thanks to Miss Henny and her legacy." Donovan whistled softly.

Bradley couldn't help but add, "And Claire Woodbury, too."

Chapter Seven

Claire retrieved Emily after her nap and carried her to the shed to get to a better stopping point on a lemonade pitcher she was making for Diane's shop. The day before, she'd run into Bradley's aunt while shopping with Emily in the Peachtree Market, and Vi had told her Diane wanted one for the display she was planning for the Art Walk. After tickling Emily's chin and recommending the blueberry cobbler from the deli in the back, Vi had waved goodbye and reminded her that she hoped to see Claire at church.

She'd promised to go the next Sunday. It'd be a good opportunity to meet new people and become reacquainted with Miss Henny's kind old friends. Vi Ainsworth certainly made Claire feel welcome to town, even if one disaster after another made it seem like updating Henny House was a constant and expensive battle. Some days she became so frustrated she forgot all about the good times she'd had there.

"Stay right here," Claire murmured to Emily as she sat her on the floor with her dollhouse, a few blocks and an action figure. The toddler's shirt was wet from a leaking sippy cup, but the afternoon heat would soon dry it up.

Claire slid onto the stool at her worktable and eyed the lump of clay she'd thrown during Emily's naptime. It didn't resemble a pitcher at all, more like a leaky cauldron. She grunted in frustration and fiddled with the edges.

"Hi!" Emily jumped up from the floor and looked outside, and Claire leaned back to look through the open doors. She was expecting to see Mr. Thu again. He'd walked over yesterday and asked permission to start a lily bed in a space along the boundary they shared in the front yard.

Claire had agreed with enthusiasm. He'd done so much for her she felt guilty. All she'd repaid him with for mowing the yard almost weekly were plates of extra cookies she baked for Emily. They often sat on the porch and ate them together with him telling her stories about his childhood in Vietnam and complaining she was spoiling him. Claire promised him he was helping her out by eating some of the extra calories she might consume while living in a stressful disaster zone.

Emily screeched in excitement again and Bradley's silhouette darkened the doorway. He looked like he'd just come from the office with his clean shirt and slim-fitting trousers. His suntanned face smiled as a spicy cologne wafted through the shed.

Claire's heart skipped a beat and a tingle radiated across her chest. "Aren't you a sight for sore eyes." She laughed, telling herself she should be over her schoolgirl reaction every time he walked into the room.

Emily lifted her arms, wanting to be held. He obeyed without hesitation and fitted her onto his hip. It looked very natural, except he was holding a pet carrier. "I told you I'd come by after naptime," he reminded them.

"The parlor floor is dry, and you were right," admitted Claire. "Redoing those floors in a darker stain was as good as replacing them, and they still look updated."

"I'm glad you like them."

Claire grinned. "They'd be good enough for Miss Henny's clogging routine if she were here to entertain us, and boy, could that woman clog."

Bradley chuckled. "And you saved money." His smile looked stilted.

Claire narrowed her eyes as something thumped in the pet carrier. "Yes, I know repairing what I have can be less expensive than changing the materials out. You don't have to remind me," she joked. "There aren't tools in that carrier, are there?"

"Tools!" parroted Emily. She patted Bradley's cheek with her damp hand now grimy with dust.

"No, not exactly," he admitted. "I'll check the parlor floors in a few minutes. First, there's something I want to talk to you about." He lowered Emily to the floor, sat in his nice pants with her and rested the pet carrier beside him. Something made a mewing noise.

"Please tell me that's a cat and not something you caught in the attic." Claire scooted off her metal stool and dropped down beside him. Emily crawled over and peeked through the carrier's tiny, grated door. She squealed with delight, and Bradley looked pleased. He caught Claire's eye, and a deep smile sank into his cheek, showing his dimple. Claire's heart did a little pirouette, but she ignored it. It was just a dimple, she sternly told herself.

"So there was an abandoned kitten that snuck into Kudzu's yesterday…" Bradley began.

Claire's mouth dropped open. She peeked over Emily and saw two dark eyes not too different than Bradley's peering out of the carrier. "You adopted a cat?"

His smile thinned. "Not exactly."

"Bradley," teased Claire, suspecting a huge favor, "what have you done?"

"They were going to call Animal Control," Bradley explained in a rush, "but he's so small and friendly, it didn't seem right. I took him home last night but can't keep him because of my rental contract."

"And you want to leave it here."

He blew out a soft puff of air at her response to his expectation. "I was hoping to give him to Emily, if you don't mind taking him in?" Bradley hesitated with a pleading look that melted Claire's heart. "I know you already have your hands full, so I'll take care of all of the expenses. I even brought kitten food."

She held up a hand to stop him as Emily poked her fingers through the front of the carrier. The kitten meowed louder then sniffed her. "Pony!" Emily shouted with delight. She was smitten. A guilty laugh burbled out of Bradley, and he met Claire's chiding look with a smidgeon of guilt. She sighed and corrected Emily. "It's a kitty."

Cats. Miss Henny always had cats. Marty, Rosy and Diana had been furry companions and affectionate friends to Claire once upon a time. "Mm'kay." She realized it wasn't a hard choice. "A kitten would be good for Emily I suppose."

"I knew you'd understand!"

Claire had to smile at Bradley's beaming relief because it lit up his whole face. He leaned over like he wanted to hug her but caught his breath and turned to fumble with the latch on the carrier instead.

Claire's cheeks flooded with warmth from a sharp moment of disappointment—and longing.

Emily broke the awkward mood. She clapped her hands with excitement and in one quick vault, the kitten leaped into her waiting hands. She squished it to her chest, an angelic smile reaching the corners of her eyes.

"That's Kudzu," Bradley informed her, petting the cat between her arms. "I'll take him to the doctor and get him all checked out for you. Can you say *Kudzu*?"

"Pony," insisted Emily. She gave her father a pout.

"Kudzu is cute," said Claire.

Bradley leaned back on one hand and slanted his head Claire's direction. "It's Pony," he repeated in mock offense.

Close enough to lean in and press her forehead to his, all Claire could think to do was chuckle. "Right." Bradley's smile softened, but his gaze deepened. Her heart burned in response then her mind scuttled backward, trying to think straight. What had he meant bringing this kitten into their lives? It was a gift, a living gift, but if she was honest with herself, she yearned for something more from him.

"Thank you," Bradley murmured, "for everything."

Claire couldn't look away. He didn't have to explain; she knew he meant it for other things besides the kitten. His stare rested on her. Claire's pulse began to gallop. A part of her mind poked her with the reminder that this had once been Dori's husband. She'd always told Claire she would like him if she met him, but neither of them had had any idea how right she'd be. Claire had feelings for Bradley in all the ways Dori had not. It was unusual, but was it okay? What would Dori say?

"So," Bradley whispered, moving his head even closer.

"Pony," sang Emily.

Claire forced herself to break the connection with the man beside her by dragging her gaze away and focusing on the newest furry member of Henny House. Bradley belonged to Emily now. Before that, he'd belonged to Dori. Claire was just the best friend, the caregiver, just like Miss Henny had once been. Or did he think of her as something more?

Bradley found going to church more enjoyable knowing Claire and Emily would be there. Just as the clock struck the hour, he peeked over his shoulder and saw them in the back row. Emily was looking around with curiosity at the many faces, and Claire was trying to recapture her attention with a small children's book. Beside her, Ms. Olivia beamed like she was thrilled to be seated next to the newest member of the congregation.

Donovan nudged Bradley and gave him a knowing look, so Bradley turned back around, but not before Aunt Vi followed his gaze and waved at Claire. Claire waved back with pink cheeks, and Bradley wondered if her darting gaze meant she was thinking about him almost kissing her in the pottery studio.

His heart simmered hungrily. Maybe he would have regretted it, but he doubted it. He caught her eye again and winked when Ms. Olivia wasn't looking, and Claire gave him a small smile that Emily interrupted when she straddled her lap and opened the book in front of her face. He hardly heard any of the sermon.

After church, Bradley parked in his usual spot behind the pharmacy and jogged up the back stairs to the loft. He only had a few minutes to change for supper since he'd dawdled with Barney on the church steps talking about a new food truck in the area. Then Diane had grabbed his arm to inform him that Daphne at the Lucky Azalea B and B wanted to update her kitchen without ruining the original floors and archways. He'd passed her his card and said hello to Emily when Claire walked past with the little girl.

Emily had thrown her arms around him right then and there, and he'd wondered what it would be like to hear her call him "Daddy," but she'd only babbled about Pony and checked his shirt pocket for snacks. He'd given her a mint, realizing he didn't care what others thought of him paying her so much attention. No one seemed to notice.

A voice was echoing from the answering machine when he reached his apartment door. Hurrying inside, Bradley tossed his Bible on a gold-plaid sofa that had seen better days and made it to the kitchen phone too late. It was Aunt Vi telling him she couldn't reach his cell phone and to bring ice cream to dinner if he had any on hand. Before he deleted it, he saw there was an older call and wondered if he needed a new cell phone company with better coverage.

"Hello, Mr. Ainsworth, this is Laurel Murphy. I'm just calling to see how restorations are going on Henny House. I drove by the other day and saw the roof is finished, but it still needs to be scraped and painted. There is a color card the historical preservation board would like to suggest. Please call me back to schedule a time to pick it up, and I will fill you in on the board's

closed-door meeting. We should be making a decision about our vacancy soon. Thank you!"

Bradley shut off the recorder. Laurel Murphy hadn't stopped him at church to ask if he'd received her message. Perhaps she'd forgotten about it. He wondered what color she had in mind for the house. Claire didn't seem the type to take instructions from a committee. He hoped to keep Henny House the lovely fresh shade of white it had been across the last three decades, but Claire had her own ideas. Regardless, it sounded like the board was close to making a decision about the available position. He didn't know the other two nominees, but he knew they were longtime residents of Kudzu Creek.

After changing from slacks into jeans, Bradley made it over to Donovan's parents' house ten minutes past Aunt Vi's invitation, with a complaining stomach. His hunger faded when he saw his father's sports car in the circular drive. It looked like Bradley hadn't been the only one invited to Sunday supper today. There were going to be conversations—conversations he wasn't ready to have. He gulped, praying they hadn't heard any rumors about Emily.

After knocking briefly, Bradley slipped inside after his aunt's greeting. Once through the front door, he found everyone seated at the dinner table under a boxy chandelier with dangling crystals.

"I thought you forgot about us," teased Aunt Vi.

His mother was beside her, in Bradley's usual seat. "I taught you better than to be late." She pursed her lips at him in disappointment.

He threw his mother his best careless grin as he slid into his chair across from his cousin. "Sorry I'm late, and no, I just ran home to change. I didn't forget." He almost wished he had.

Dad smiled at him from across the table. Without skipping a beat, Aunt Vi pierced a piece of chicken with fervor. "I saw Claire Woodbury at church today. How's the Henny project coming along?"

"Yes, the Henny House," Dad said with interest. "That's the strange Victorian house in town?"

"You would be right," said Uncle Harold.

"It's coming," Bradley assured them, and his heart thunked to his feet at the sudden turn in the conversation. He slid a concerned glance across the table toward Donovan. It wasn't the right time to talk about Claire or Emily in front of his parents. Not yet.

"The roof and porch are finished, and the parlor floor is done," Bradley said. "I've almost convinced her to paint the outside a shade of yellow instead of a crazy purple, but I'm really hoping she'll stick with the white. Her neighbors have helped clean up the yard."

"That's so exciting," Aunt Vi said approvingly. "What about the front door? I suggested she paint it a wheat color, and she said she'd think about it."

"Knowing Claire, it will probably be something trendy," Bradley replied. Saying her name in front of his parents felt tentative on his tongue.

"Black would look classic," pointed out his mother, although she probably didn't know for certain which house they were talking about.

"Paint it red," Donovan suggested with a wink.

"If she's going to live there with the little girl, I suspect she won't want to alarm the neighborhood," warned Uncle Harold. "It won't go over well with Ms. Olivia."

Bradley managed a smile. "Ms. Olivia walks by

about every other afternoon, but we haven't discussed door colors yet."

"But a purple house?" complained Mother. She caught Aunt Vi's eye, wrinkled her nose, then turned to Bradley. "I can't believe you'd rather hammer and nail and paint old houses instead of having a real career."

The table fell silent and Bradley twisted the fork in his hand while he counted to ten inside his head. "Claire is the one who's going to live there," he reminded them all, "and she has very good taste." He ignored Mother's wound-picking and fought the urge to spill everything about the chance he had to get on the historical board, and by the way, he had a child. Maybe the good news would offset the bad.

But was either really bad news? Claire had agreed to let Emily spend Sundays with him once the project was finished. That meant he would bring her to dinners at Aunt Vi and Uncle Harold's. Eventually, his parents would show up again.

Bradley's heart clomped like someone was clogging on his chest. As much as he knew his family would be shocked he had a little girl, maybe now was the best time to let the cat out of the bag after all. He thought of Emily petting her new kitten with tenderness and realized Claire was right. Emily was a blessing, not something to be kept secret. In a way, Bradley would always have a part of Dori in his life to replace the piece of his heart she'd taken with her.

"Is something wrong, Bradley?" Aunt Vi interrupted Uncle Harold's story to his brother about moles tunneling under the clubhouse golf course. "You look a little emotional."

Mother was staring at him with suspicion, as if she

HARLEQUIN® Reader Service —Here's how it works:

Accepting your 2 free books and 2 free gifts (gifts valued at approximately $10.00 retail) places you under no obligation to buy anything. You may keep the books and gifts and return the shipping statement marked "cancel." If you do not cancel, approximately one month later we'll send you 6 more books from each series you have chosen, and bill you at our low, subscribers-only discount price. Love Inspired® Romance Larger-Print books and Love Inspired® Suspense Larger-Print books consist of 6 books each month and cost just $5.99 each in the U.S. or $6.24 each in Canada. That is a savings of at least 17% off the cover price. It's quite a bargain! Shipping and handling is just 50¢ per book in the U.S. and $1.25 per book in Canada*. You may return any shipment at our expense and cancel at any time — or you may continue to receive monthly shipments at our low, subscribers-only discount price plus shipping and handling. *Terms and prices subject to change without notice. Prices do not include sales taxes which will be charged (if applicable) based on your state or country of residence. Canadian residents will be charged applicable taxes. Offer not valid in Quebec. Books received may not be as shown. All orders subject to approval. Credit or debit balances in a customer's account(s) may be offset by any other outstanding balance owed by or to the customer. Please allow 3 to 4 weeks for delivery. Offer available while quantities last. **Your Privacy** – Your information is being collected by Harlequin Enterprises ULC, operating as Harlequin Reader Service. For a complete summary of the information we collect, how we use this information and to whom it is disclosed, please visit our privacy notice located at https://corporate.harlequin.com/privacy-notice. From time to time we may also exchange your personal information with reputable third parties. If you wish to opt out of this sharing of your personal information, please visit www.readerservice.com/consumerschoice or call 1-800-873-8635. **Notice to California Residents** – Under California law, you have specific rights to control and access your data. For more information on these rights and how to exercise them, visit https://corporate.harlequin.com/california-privacy.

If offer card is missing write to: Harlequin Reader Service, P.O. Box 1341, Buffalo, NY 14240-8531 or visit www.ReaderService.com

were expecting terrible news. Her automatic response to be disappointed in him made him sad. Donovan snuck a small glance at him with concern, as if knowing what he wanted to do. Bradley realized he was right. They couldn't ruin Aunt Vi's family dinner tonight. "It's nothing," he replied. He would need to talk to his parents in private. When the time was right. He gulped, wondering what Dori must have gone through carrying her secrets alone.

"You're not falling for the girl at Henny House are you?" teased Uncle Harold.

Mother jerked her head up from over her plate and her knife slipped from her grip, clattering against the china. Bradley felt his father looking him up and down. "Um, no, of course not," he stammered. He felt his face flush and squeezed his fork, horrified to be caught off guard.

"The one who wants a purple house?" his mother repeated.

"Who is this woman?" Dad demanded.

"Oh!" said Vi with a flap of her hand. "Claire used to live here years ago. Now, she's moved back to Henny House and has a foster child."

"Interesting," murmured Bradley's father, watching him like a hawk.

Bradley concentrated on his dinner.

"Sounds like an orphanage," murmured Mother.

"She's lovely," insisted Aunt Vi, "and she's an artist. We have brunch now and then at Southern Fried Kudzu."

Bradley cleared his throat and glanced at his cousin. Donovan lifted his chin in a silent promise that he had his back. "Let me tell you about this case I had to turn down," Donovan interrupted, with a tone that promised a good story.

* * *

Bradley claimed he was full after the main course and fled out to the back deck pretending to be more interested in pondering the late afternoon sunshine than cake. He sighed with relief when he heard a car rev its engine on the other side of the house. Aunt Vi stepped outside and quietly shut the door behind her. "Are you going to come in and have dessert?"

"Are they gone?"

"You should have come in and said goodbye," his aunt chided him.

Bradley raised a shoulder, stung by the chastisement. "They could have come out and told me they were leaving."

Aunt Vi frowned as she joined him on the deck. The sun hung low in the sky but was just high enough over the trees to turn their crowns orange-gold. Cicadas buzzed in harmony. Bradley stopped pacing and leaned against the deck railing with the scenic view behind him. "I didn't want to upset anyone anymore."

"What? Bradley!" She threw her arms around his shoulders. "No one's upset. I'm certainly not. You're amazing at what you do. Your mother just has to vocalize her feelings. She'll figure it out someday."

He took a deep breath, hugged his aunt back then pulled away and returned to his post against the deck's rail. "I had something else to say, but I couldn't get the nerve up."

Aunt Vi put her hands on her hips. "What's that? You can tell me."

"Are you sure?" he asked, gathering his courage. He realized Aunt Vi was as trustworthy as his cousin. She wouldn't pick up the phone and call his parents, although that was exactly what his mother would do if the roles were reversed.

Aunt Vi nodded. "What's wrong, honey? I can tell something's been bothering you the last few weeks."

Bradley took a deep breath. "It's about Claire and the baby. Emily." Curiosity flickered in Aunt Vi's eyes, but she waited patiently. He gulped again. "She's mine."

"Claire?"

"No, just Emily," Bradley explained. His aunt's eyes widened in shock. "Didn't see that coming, huh?"

"No." She looked up at him, her nose almost to his chin. "But how?"

"Dori was her mother. Dori was Claire's best friend." He watched the puzzle pieces come together on his aunt's face.

"I see now, and I suspect Donovan knew about it by the way he behaved at dinner."

Bradley nodded. "I thought I might need a lawyer or at least some advice. I will eventually."

"How long have you known?" Aunt Vi's forehead creased, and he gripped the rail behind him. This was coming out easier than expected.

"I figured it out almost as soon as they moved in. Claire had pictures of Dori, and I learned they were college roommates. Dori moved back to Birmingham to live with her after…after she left me."

"I see," said Aunt Vi slowly. "So she never told you?"

"No." Bradley's shoulders slumped. "She should have. To keep something like this away from me is just…" He wiped his brow. "Well, it's almost unforgivable. Breaking up with me was one thing, but this…"

"Oh, honey, you're going to have to forgive her someday. Besides, I'm sure she would have told you eventually. Does anyone else know? Her parents?"

"Yes, they do. She told them before she died, but they wouldn't hear of it. I guess that's why they never spoke to Mother or Dad again, not just because of the elopement but because they knew there was a baby."

Aunt Vi put a hand to her heart. "My word, who would do such a thing? How ridiculous. You and Dori made your own choices, before and after, and I'm sure you would have stayed friends. She was a part of your life for so many years, and you went through so much together."

"Yes, and I get some of it." Bradley took a breath. "Although she still should have told me. She cut off contact because of Emily. Maybe she thought I would have given everything up and come home."

"You would have," murmured Aunt Vi. She looked at Bradley knowingly. "Dori loved you so much she didn't want you to miss out on your dream, especially after you stood up to your parents to chase it."

Bradley winced. "She still shouldn't have kept it from me," he insisted, trying to hold back the anger he'd fought for so long.

"Yes, I agree. She shouldn't have. But we can't all see the end of the road when we're standing in a ditch with everyone criticizing us for how we got there." Aunt Vi moved beside Bradley and clasped her hands over the railing. She stared into the sun. "I bet if Dori was as wonderful a girl as you say, she would have told you as soon as she was ready or thought you were."

"I'll never know," Bradley whispered.

Aunt Vi tore her gaze away from the oncoming dusk.

"You will someday, and you need to forgive her. What about Claire?"

"She didn't know I was here, but she's been honest with me. I can tell she loves Emily like her own flesh and blood."

"This must be excruciating for her, and yet she's let you into their lives."

"Well, her house, anyway," allowed Bradley.

Aunt Vi cocked her head at him. "So do you think of Claire like you would a sister, too, or is there something more?"

Bradley felt his cheeks flood with warmth even as the blood in his chest seemed to shower down to his fingertips. "I'm pretty sure I don't think of Claire as a sister," he assured her. "I'd be in a whole lot of trouble if I did. But we're just friends." A friend that he wanted to kiss, he thought.

"Well," Aunt Vi mused, "I'm sure Dori wouldn't mind. She'd probably be as pleased as punch."

He looked at her in surprise. "Do you really think so?"

She clasped her hands and brought them to her chin. "Bradley, if my brother had fallen in love with my best friend growing up, I would have been the happiest girl on earth."

"Oh, no," he blurted, "it's not love. I just admire her. I mean, she's wonderful, and I like her a lot, but that doesn't mean anything. She is—was—Dori's best friend. I couldn't..."

"Why not?" Aunt Vi slapped him playfully on the shoulder. "I guess we'll have to see then, won't we? For now, let's go inside and have cake and talk about Emily and when I get to play with her. No more secrets."

Bradley relented with a smile. The word was out. How long it took to spread through Kudzu Creek he wasn't sure, but one thing was for certain, he'd better work up the courage to tell his parents soon—before they learned about it from someone other than their own son.

Chapter Eight

Much to Claire's amusement, Bradley acted like he'd hit a home run after he talked her into a yellowy taupe shade of exterior paint for Henny House. It was called Dayroom Yellow, and she rather liked it. It would contrast nicely with all of the bright green shrubbery growing around it.

Bradley and the crew he'd hired to refurbish some of the wood floors were finally finishing up, and a new handyman had been hired to lay Italian tile in the main bath downstairs. The original tiny octagon tiles on the floor were carefully pulled up in large pieces, and Bradley sent them to a warehouse outside of town until they could be used for another project.

The weather grew searing, even for Kudzu Creek, so Claire pushed her pottery time to the evening and made other plans. She buckled Emily into the stroller after Bradley stopped working long enough to kiss her little cheek. Claire found herself standing too close and feeling a little envious, so she stared at the floor rather than meet his searching eyes after he told Emily goodbye.

Bradley hadn't said a word about almost kissing

Claire in the shed or about what it meant and how he felt. Perhaps he'd just been caught up in the moment, filled with gratitude for all she'd done for Emily. He'd only said thank you, after all.

Deciding, at the very least, they would be close friends, Claire ambled down the sidewalk with Emily to meet Diane for lunch at Kudzu's. Vi Ainsworth had told Diane that Emily was Bradley's and Dori's daughter, and she wanted to know more. Diane hadn't known Claire's best friend personally, but regardless, Claire was just happy Bradley had told someone.

"Hello! Hello, there!"

Claire stopped and turned to find Ms. Olivia straining to catch up with her. "Good morning, Ms. Olivia. Are you heading into town this morning?"

"Me? Oh, no. The market drops off my groceries for me once a week." Ms. Olivia puffed beside her. Her wig had fallen over her forehead, and she mindlessly pushed it back. "I just wanted to say good morning. I don't see you on your front porch very much."

"I have a pottery studio in the back," Claire explained.

"Is that where you spend all your time?" the woman said in wonder before she seemed to remember her mission. "Well, I just thought you'd want to know I saw a small cat nosing around your front porch yesterday. I tried to call you, but you must have been in your studio."

"Oh, that's Emily's new cat. Her father—" Claire caught herself. "I mean, Bradley Ainsworth gave it to her."

"Her father?" asked Ms. Olivia in surprise. She hadn't missed a word.

Claire gave an uneasy laugh. "It's kind of a personal situation," she hinted, "and complicated."

"Oh, I understand," her neighbor said slowly, "a family thing. The poor dear."

"Yes, a family situation," said Claire in a rush, wondering if it was Emily or Bradley who was the poor dear. "You'll have to ask him about it yourself."

"Oh, no use bothering him." Ms. Olivia smiled. She gave Emily a momentary study then pulled her head back as if seeing Claire for the first time. "What a good soul you are, Claire," she declared, "much like your Miss Henny."

"Thank you." Claire meant it. "I better get Emily to our lunch date before she gets crabby."

"Of course." Ms. Olivia waved her on. "And don't worry about my gelatin bowl. I'll come pick it up sometime when you're not busy."

Claire chuckled and waved goodbye. Of course Ms. Olivia wouldn't mind stopping by again, but it was Claire's fault. She should have already returned it. She watched Ms. Olivia toddle back toward her house, wave at a passing car then continue on her way. Claire was beginning to feel like a local in town strolling Emily around a few times a week. It gave her a profound sense of security she'd never felt living in Birmingham.

Mac was always working in the diner when Claire wandered in, and the server shared the same love of historical fiction that she did. Barney often stuck his head around the corner and asked about Pony, which led to baby talk with Emily, and then Diane was just a couple of doors down. Sometimes Mr. Thu was just leaving Kudzu's with his Reuben sandwich and French fries, and twice he'd sat and eaten with them, sharing his booty with Emily who preferred fried potatoes over fruit cups.

The sky over Kudzu Creek looked as blue as the water at the seashore, and there was hardly a cloud in the sky. Birds twittered from the eaves of the shops. Green banners fluttered from the lampposts in the mild breeze announcing the date of the upcoming city Art Walk. Emily sang a nursery rhyme and rocked back and forth in the stroller.

Claire parked the buggy, grabbed Emily's hand and walked inside Kudzu's. Diane was waiting for them with a tall glass of hibiscus lemonade on the table. "Hi, baby!" she called to Emily, and the toddler grinned. Claire led her to the counter and ordered a salad to share with a side of turmeric rice in case Emily balked at a plate of vegetables.

Diane received her order just as Claire and Emily took two chairs at the little table beside her. "Your blue fruit bowl sold," Diane announced when Claire sat down. "Laurel bought it, after all." She chuckled as if this were a joke.

Claire beamed. "That's wonderful news. I have a half dozen cruets drying."

"Great." Diane picked up a celery stick stuffed with pimento cheese and bit into it. "The pitchers don't seem to move as well as I thought they would, but the cruets and your fruit bowls go pretty fast. Are you ready for the Art Walk yet?"

"You mean besides cruets to fill with your oils?" Claire smiled. "I have four more bowls. Two have already been fired."

"What color?"

Claire smiled. "You'll have to wait and see."

Mac brought Claire's order over, and she thanked her then settled Emily on her knees with a carrot stick and slice of cucumber. Diane set her glass down with a clap and waved toward the front door. When Claire looked up, Laurel from the historical preservation board and chamber of commerce snaked over. She was wearing the same type of outfit Claire had seen her wear before: professional slacks, silk blouse, skinny heels and chunky, expensive-looking jewelry.

"Diane, are you ready for the Art Walk yet?"

"We were just talking about it." Diane motioned toward Claire. "We're going to have a table outside the front door with new artists, and Claire's pottery will be in the left window."

Laurel glanced at Claire. "I'm sure that will be very nice." She looked to the counter then seemed to change her mind. "Do you care if I sit for a moment? I'm here to pick up lunch for the chamber, and it's probably not ready yet." She pulled out the fourth chair before Diane or Claire could respond. "So," she sang, folding her hands in her lap and dodging Emily's flapping carrot stick. "I understand Henny House is about to undergo a facelift. The outside is ready for paint?"

Claire looked at her curiously. "It's still under renovation, but yes, soon." She smiled like the constant mess and strangers going in and out did not make things difficult.

As if reading her mind, Diane offered, "It'll be worth it in the end. I can't wait to see your new floor in the bathroom."

"Oh, yes?" questioned Laurel. "What did you do? Clean the tile? Replace the grout?" Before Claire could reply, Laurel leaned forward to Diane. "Have you seen the copper tub at the resale store outside of town? They pulled it from the Blankenship farmhouse."

"Sounds charming," Diane relented. "In fact, that'd be a cool feature in my shop. I could fill it with books and bath bombs."

Laurel looked horrified. She turned back to Claire. "What about your tile?"

Claire grit her teeth for a second then answered. "We actually pulled the tile off the floors and the walls. My installer is laying a beige Italian tile called Tuscan Sand."

"An earthy-toned Italian tile in Henny House?" groaned Laurel. "Besides restoring the original wood floors, I would have thought you would have used something more reminiscent of the period when it came to tile."

Flushing, Claire informed her, "I kept the original floors in the foyer, parlor and upstairs. Everything else is new."

"You mean rescued." Laurel's stern voice held hope.

"No," rallied Claire, offended that she could not express herself in the house Miss Henny had left her. "Fresh from the home improvement store in Columbus."

"That's unfortunate," Laurel answered in a tone that signified she found it atrocious. "You can't be a historic landmark if you destroy a house with cheap retail materials." She looked aghast and then in a bitter tone added, "I suppose that's why I haven't heard back from Bradley Ainsworth. He hasn't returned my calls."

Claire took a bite of salad to keep her mouth busy. Laurel dug around in her designer purse that was sure to be an original and pushed a paint sample card across the table. It was green with red accents. Claire examined it, but let Diane pick it up.

"What's this?" Diane asked.

"It's my recommendation to Mr. Ainsworth for the exterior of Henny House." Laurel looked at Claire meaningfully. Claire swallowed her salad and took a long drink of water.

"It's nice," said Diane. She held it in front of Claire. "What do you think? Very appropriate, although I have to admit it doesn't look like your taste."

Claire gave a small shake of her head. "I actually have something different in mind." She suddenly wished she had stuck with eggplant purple instead of downgrading to a soft yellow.

"Yes?" Laurel leaned forward with dread-filled eyes just as Emily waved her arm around again. A half-eaten slimy cucumber slice slapped Laurel in the ear. "Ugh!" she exclaimed as Claire reached for the toddler's hand.

"Sit down, Emily," Claire chided her. "Keep your food on your napkin." Aware she'd done something wrong, Emily settled low in the chair and scooted closer to Claire.

Laurel wiped off the point of impact with a napkin Diane offered her. "I wish they had high chairs in here," Laurel blustered in a high voice, "so children can be strapped down."

"She has to wear a safety belt in her stroller," Claire explained, "so I don't mind letting her learn to sit and eat properly when we're inside. Most people don't seem to mind."

Laurel clearly did mind. She wiped at her silk blouse as if it'd been affected, too. "I suppose it is the best way to teach manners," she muttered. She glanced at Emily from the corner of her eye. "She's a foster child, I understand, not your real daughter, so she'll move on eventually? I hope for your sake you don't get too attached, being a single woman and all. Are you trying to continue Miss Henny's legacy? How many more do you think there'll be?"

Claire paused, overwhelmed at all of the questions. Was she continuing Miss Henny's legacy? Not intentionally. Emily was like her own child, if she had one, she realized. She loved this little girl with all of her heart. She couldn't bear the thought of replacing her.

"She's as good as my own," Claire declared, although her heart ached inside knowing she was not. Not really. The thought of Emily not being in her life was an ice pick to the soul, but she calmed herself. Bradley had promised he wouldn't keep them apart, no matter what the future held.

"Actually," intervened Diane, "Emily is local. I'm sure she'll be staying in Kudzu Creek for as long as Bradley Ainsworth and Claire wish her to."

Laurel's forehead crinkled. "Why?"

Diane reached across the table and handed a cracker to Emily, who took it greedily. "Snack," she replied with pleasure.

Claire couldn't help but hold back a smile of pride. She met Laurel's wide-eyed gaze. "I plan on settling here, and Emily will always be a part of my life."

"Is Emily Bradley Ainsworth's child?" Laurel gasped in a scandalized tone.

"Yes," responded Claire with a cringe. She wondered if Bradley would be upset word had begun to spread. Rather than share any details because she was certain it wouldn't appease the woman, she added, "He doesn't have custody right now, but we're working on that."

Laurel's lips pruned. She pushed back from the table. "No custody? I can't imagine what he's done. I knew he was related to Harold and Viola, but not that he had a…a homeless child." She sniffed.

"She's not homeless," Claire nipped back, her temper ignited, "and she isn't motherless or fatherless, not that it's anyone's business."

Diane made a soothing sound. "Emily's a beautiful little girl. I'm sure she's lucky to have you, Claire," she remarked.

"For the time being." Laurel looked at the green paint card on the tabletop. "Please do consider the paint recommendation from the historical preservation board," she instructed Claire in a terse tone. "We don't want Henny House to be a blemish on the community." With a sideways glance at Emily, she nodded at Diane, who gave her a small wave, then strode up to the counter for her takeout order. Diane rolled her eyes at her back.

Claire passed Emily a cup of dressing to dip her cracker in. The baby looked up at her with gratitude. "Can you say thank you?" Claire reminded her.

Emily grinned. "I love you," she sang.

"I love you, too," Claire whispered back. She did, she realized, more than anything in the world—even more than Henny House and Kudzu Creek.

Diane chuckled. "Don't mind Laurel," she murmured. "She likes to think she runs the town, but she cares. She really does. She has all the respect in the world for the Hennys and the Ainsworths. She just doesn't like change—or surprises."

"I don't know why Emily having a parent here is such a surprise. Would she rather me raise her on the other side of the country?"

"I don't think it's really that." Diane lowered her

voice. "Bradley wasn't the only one interested in buying Henny House."

"That makes a little more sense," Claire acknowledged. "I knew there were some showings when the house was on the market. She must have had a look."

"She's very passionate," Diane allowed.

"Too bad I'm not going anywhere, and I don't like that shade of green," Claire replied. She pondered Laurel's remarks about Bradley having a child. "And Bradley Ainsworth is a wonderful, kind and responsible man." She knew it with every atom of her being, just as Dori had known it, too.

Bradley paced the family law office Donovan had recommended. He shot a glimpse at Claire across the waiting room. She was reading a magazine as if she didn't have a care in the world, but the leg she'd crossed over the other bounced up and down like she felt anxious, too. Bradley wandered over and plopped down beside her where he'd started out. Her small hand dropped from the magazine onto his leg. "It's going to be okay," she promised him with a light pat. His heart calmed and tingled at the edges, but before he could take her hand into his, she slid it away.

Right. This was business. He folded his arms over his chest and squared his shoulders. "I'm just so nervous," he murmured, although there was no one else in the room except the receptionist behind the counter.

Claire looked up from the French toast recipe she was reading. "It's going to be fine. They have the DNA results, and I wrote everything out and had it notarized." She gave him a little smile, but there was telltale color splotched on her cheeks. "This is just an interview, and they'll tell us how to proceed."

"Are you okay?" Bradley leaned close to whisper in her ear. "I know you love her—Emily, and all, but..."

Claire deflected with a, "We'll figure those things out later." She returned to the magazine and ignored him. Was it on purpose? Was she really afraid of losing Emily?

"We should have talked about it," Bradley conceded, "before coming here. Your *long-term* expectations. Mine." There were a lot of things they hadn't discussed. Claire always acted so cheerful while she was on the go, but it seemed she kept a part of herself reserved behind a wall of solid rock. She'd said nothing after he'd almost kissed her in her studio. She'd also changed the subject whenever he'd wondered aloud how Emily would do in his loft above the pharmacy.

"When the house is finished..." he began again.

Claire looked up from her magazine. She was so close, he wanted to lean over and kiss her pert full lips. Bradley glanced at the silent receptionist and breathed impatiently.

"I think I can handle the rest of the paint inside," Claire said conversationally. "The outside is another thing."

Bradley mumbled, "Mmm-hmm," but it was not at all what he wanted to talk about. Did she know he had feelings for her? Thinking about her when he was alone made him light-headed. Being with her in the same house even though they stayed busy with different projects made him feel at home, or at least, like he was in a place he was meant to be. "It looks amazing inside," he complimented her. "You know I wish we'd kept the original floors in the kitchen, but I understand you wanted something more durable."

"At least we didn't pull them up," pointed out Claire. "They're still underneath should anyone want to see them someday."

He gave a quiet chuckle. "So, about the exterior paint..."

She gave him a teasing grin. "You sold me on the yellow. Please don't try to talk me into what the historical board wants. It's Henny House, not the Chamber of Commerce."

Bradley laughed. "You're a Henny through and through, aren't you? You sure know what you want once you make up your mind."

"I have to," Claire explained. "As a child, I learned pretty quickly no one else was going to fight for me. So, if I really wanted something, I had to dig in my heels and find a way."

"Well, you've certainly found a way with Henny House." Bradley nudged her with his elbow. "We just need to decide on the gazebo."

"Ugh," she grumbled. On this, neither one of them would budge.

"Have you ever had tea on a nice afternoon and just sat there to watch the neighborhood?"

"No," Claire mumbled, "but Laurel Murphy's grandmother has."

Bradley chuckled again. "Did you know the word 'gazebo' comes from the mid-eighteenth century? It means 'I shall gaze.'"

She looked up with interest. "I did not."

He studied her little face. "Yes, and they were built by civilizations as early as the Egyptians."

"I like Egyptian history," Claire admitted.

On a roll, Bradley continued. "It's also similar to the French term *Que c'est beau*."

"What's that mean?"

He stared at her deeply. "How beautiful."

Claire's cheeks colored, and she shifted her gaze back to the magazine. "I still think the gazebo needs to go," she stammered in a halting tone. "It is nice on its own accord, but it's odd to have it hanging off one end of the porch. I need the house to look symmetrical. Perfect."

Bradley pursed his lips. "But real life isn't symmetrical or perfect. Maybe you wouldn't find it odd if you used it more often."

"I don't use it all," she argued.

He grimaced. "I don't think I can do it, Claire. It would break my heart and be completely at odds with what I do as a preservationist." His frown became a sigh. "Not to mention there's what the historical preservation board would think, if I'm being completely honest."

"Mr. Ainsworth?"

They both jumped.

Bradley scrambled to his feet with jerky movements and wished he could take Claire's hand, but that would look odd. She was the guardian of his child and nothing more, except a very good friend, a trusted friend, like Dori had been. His heart sank with disappointment. Maybe Dori and Claire were more similar than he knew. Tearing down the beautiful gazebo because it was imperfect was probably a sign. He should set aside these growing feelings for her before he got his heart broken again.

They followed the receptionist into the office and found the lawyer waiting for them. The woman offered her hand with a smile that radiated confidence and encouragement. After greeting her, Bradley sank into one of the plush leather chairs on the other side of the desk, with Claire sitting stiffly beside him. He saw her hand drop to her side and resisted reaching for it if only to give her a little squeeze of thanks.

"You'll be happy to know the test results validate your statements," began the attorney. Bradley felt a light weight float off the top of his shoulders. He reached for Claire's hand, after all, but only brushed against it when he found it fisted. It felt as cold as ice.

First Dori. Then Miss Henny. Now Emily. Claire's body felt wooden for the second day in a row as she moved through the house. Although it was coming together beautifully, she felt like a funeral was just around the corner. Going to the lawyer had been the next step and the right thing to do, but someday Emily wouldn't belong to her anymore.

The sound of two men laying tile in the upstairs second bathroom echoed off the ceiling. Finished with the breakfast dishes, she wandered to the bedroom down the hall that Emily and she shared. She could hear Bradley's soft laughter and Emily's high-pitched giggles. He'd arrived during her breakfast with his work crew, and after directing some repairs on the cornices outside, had let himself in to play with his daughter.

When Claire rounded the corner, Bradley and Emily were not in the bedroom littered with blankets and toys like she'd expected. Pony was curled up alone on the bed, dozing. She picked him up, and he stretched in her arms. His eyes had turned green and looked as round as nickels. "Where's your baby girl?" she wondered aloud.

Emily's laughter pealed again. It was a deep and effervescent sound soaked with happiness. Pony scrambled to get out of her arms, and Claire dropped him to the floor. She cocked an ear to listen. The laughter was coming from outside on the porch.

Claire snatched a bobby pin off the nightstand and pinned her lengthening bangs over her ear. She listened to the deep musical tones of Bradley's voice, and a wave of longing washed over her. Just hearing him made her feel guarded, as if he might mesmerize her into believing things that were impossible. There was a motherless child between them, and Claire needed to think and act like Miss Henny if she wanted to do what was best for her friend's daughter.

More gurgling laughter came through the windows, and Claire sauntered back through the house to check the front yard. She pretended, just for a moment, that she could see Miss Henny sitting in the parlor with a book in her hand. The imaginary apparition looked up and smiled at Claire then pointed toward the porch.

Claire nodded although Miss Henny wasn't actually there. Leaving parts of the house untouched, just cleaning them up and restoring some of the damage here and there, made it feel like yesterday wasn't so long ago. It kept Miss Henny's memory alive, Claire realized, and she needed that connection. The faint growl of thunder sounded from far away. She hurried to open the front door and looked out in concern. The yard was vacant except for some scaffolding covered by a tarp.

The porch boards vibrated underneath her feet, and more merriment floated through the air.

Claire checked the gazebo at the end of the porch and found her missing baby and good-looking contractor. Bradley was dancing around with Emily's bare feet planted on the toes of his boots. Her little fingers gripped his with the confidence of a two-year-old as they twirled around in circles, making her giggle. They were so lost in their daddy-daughter dance, they must not have noticed the weather. A wide smile on Bradley's face made his dimple show, and his brown eyes were tapered with affection as he looked down at his little girl.

He loved her, Claire realized. It was new and fresh, and maybe not as deep as Claire's love because she'd had Emily longer, but there was something pure and devoted in his expression. He would love her as much as Dori had. In that moment, Claire knew it and allowed herself to accept that, for now, everything would be okay. Looking around at all of the work he'd done on the house, especially the updates he hadn't agreed with, she knew Bradley was a man of his word. She hadn't met many people like him in all her years alone.

Claire strolled down the porch to join them. The gingerbread trim around the top of the gazebo was flaked and rotting and two pieces were missing on a section that faced the road. Strangely, it didn't make the scene any less charming. "What are you two doing?"

"We're practicing our dancing."

"In the gazebo?"

"That's what they're for. Don't you watch old movies?"

Claire chuckled and dropped onto the bench built along the hexagon edges of the gazebo. "No, but I bet you do." Bradley spun by, stopped and plopped Emily down on the bench, and grabbed Claire by both hands.

"Oh no, I—"

Before she knew it, Claire was spinning around the gazebo in Bradley's arms. He was quite debonair and knew what he was doing. She laughed as their twirling motion pulled back her head. Bradley drew her close, his hand warm on her waist as rain began to spatter the rooftop.

"Uh-oh!" cried Emily.

"It's okay, we'll stay dry," Bradley assured her.

Emily clapped her hands with glee as he and Claire whirled by. "I guess they won't start painting in the back today with this weather," Claire said.

"And no one can tear down this lovely thing," Bradley added. "I'm sorry I can't bring myself to do it. Have you thought about opening the wall in the back of the study and putting in French doors to have access here?"

Claire's mind was whirling, and being so close to Bradley with his arms around her waist made her heart spin like a top, too. She suddenly could see herself getting up from a laptop situated on Miss Henny's father's cherry-stained desk and pushing open a glass door to walk outside to the porch. "No, and it's not a terrible idea," she admitted, but she didn't confess the idea of quick access to the gazebo would be nice if it remained. She still hadn't found another crew to do it.

Bradley spun her around one last time then dipped her with a flourish that left them nose to nose. Claire forgot about construction projects and drew in a gasp, but whether she was breathless because of their dancing or because his chest was pressed against hers, she wasn't sure. He smelled like soap and pine, and it made her mouth water. She swallowed and stared into his eyes, mesmerized.

The smile on his face froze, but she watched it slowly

melt as his gaze pierced her heart like no one else's had ever done. Thunder complained again, louder this time, and Emily gave a high-pitched shriek. Claire forced herself back to reality and looked away. In unspoken agreement, Bradley pulled her to her feet, and she dropped his hands. They both turned to the toddler, and Claire held out her arms as she wondered if Bradley's pulse was racing, too. Was he trembling with the same yearning she felt? She tossed her head to clear it.

"Come here, baby," she cooed to Emily.

One of the tile installers popped his head out the front door and looked their way. "Mr. Ainsworth," he called over the rain.

Bradley cleared his throat, either to excuse himself or dispel the moment. Claire wasn't sure which. He gave a small wave to the man. Their conversation was drowned out by torrential rainfall.

Emily squealed and laughed, raising her arms to shield herself from mist thrown up by the pounding raindrops on the sides of the gazebo. Claire laughed and spun her around slowly, singing her favorite nursery rhyme. The gazebo protected them from the rain, and Claire smiled to herself knowing with the new roof on the house it would be just as dry and secure inside. Safe. Cozy.

Emily dropped her head onto Claire's shoulder, and peace fell over them as they swayed to the rhythm of the rain. Realizing the baby was nodding off, Claire pressed a hand against her little back and crossed the repaired porch, noticing patches where the old railing had been removed. The columns had a fresh coat of white primer. She smiled to herself and walked inside knowing Emily would have a good nap, which would leave her extra time to get more things done. Bradley bounded down the staircase, and she stopped in surprise at his hurry and the pensive look on his face.

"What is it?" Claire asked when he reached the bottom stair.

He forced a smile that Claire could see right through. "It's the plumbing," he answered in a reluctant tone.

Claire's stomach twisted, but she clung to the hope that it was just a minor thing like so many of the other problems in the house besides the termite damage and the roof. "How much?"

He wagged his head sorrowfully, his gaze darting between her and Emily's blond locks. "I'm sorry, Claire. The pipes upstairs aren't up to code, and some show signs of leaking. They'll all have to be replaced. We'll have to open up the walls."

She gasped in disappointment. "All of them?"

"Upstairs in that bathroom, yes. I'm sorry, but..." He shifted his stance and toed a knot in the floor that caught his interest. "It looks like there's been leaking from the bathtub spigots for years, and they can't lay any tile until all of the wood beneath the floor is replaced."

Dollar signs multiplied in a long row before Claire's eyes like dancing elephants. "But we were almost done! I don't have a lot of cash left. You know the budget."

"Yes." Bradley sounded sorrowful. "It'll take all of it, and it may not be enough." He gave a sharp sigh.

Nausea erupted in Claire's tight stomach and she wished she hadn't eaten eggs for breakfast. Heat dampened her forehead. She squeezed her eyes shut and tried to think. "The shed—I mean the studio. We don't have to repair the roof or put in new flooring out there, and

I don't need new furniture for the house right away, either. I'll keep Miss Henny's sofas and chaise and worry about that another day."

Bradley made a noise, and she knew, without him saying anything, that that still wouldn't cover it. "We could save the tiles upstairs," she suggested, forcing her eyes open to face the obvious. "I don't have to have new flooring up there. All of the wood floors in the hall and other rooms are staying anyway."

"That would probably do it." Bradley's voice held encouragement. "And I've already paid for the exterior paint, so..."

Claire nodded her head and tried to look confident. "Do what you have to do. I'm going to put Emily down for a nap."

"I'm sorry. I wish I had better news."

"I know you do." Claire offered him a brave smile but fought back tears of frustration forming behind her eyes. He watched her for a moment then surprised her by brushing a kiss across her cheek. "It'll be okay." He turned and headed back upstairs.

Claire carried Emily to their bedroom down the hall, her cheek tingling with pleasure. It was funny how a friendly kiss could dance all the way down to your toes. She nibbled her lip, unsure of how much more friendly she should feel toward Bradley with him beside her almost every day.

Emily snuggled her face into Claire's neck, and she forced herself to shake off her own desires and concentrate on the problem at hand. No money left meant she needed her pottery to sell and sell well. If that didn't work out, she'd have to find a job outside the house.

That meant fewer hours in the studio, and worse, less time with Emily.

Claire's eyes would have brimmed over with tears of disappointment if Bradley's lingering peck on the cheek did not still warm her. What did it matter? she realized sadly. It wasn't like she would have to get a babysitter for Emily. Loft apartment or not, she would soon be turned over to her father.

Chapter Nine

Bradley worked outside the next two days, directing the painting crew in the backyard in between running upstairs to the bathroom to watch the plumbers switch out the old pipes. Frustrated with the rising costs of repairs and updates, Claire seemed near despondent at times, but in other moments, she was her usual cheerful self, chasing Emily around on her trike or busy in the pottery studio. She didn't mention him brushing a kiss across her cheek, but she hadn't seemed to mind it. It was all Bradley could do to stop himself from offering more.

He waited until late afternoon after the workers left to corner her in the kitchen. Aunt Vi had invited Claire to Sunday dinner, and she'd declined, citing the work left to do to prepare for the biannual Art Walk in town.

Bradley knew Claire could not be any more ready for the next weekend. It felt like the closer he came to receiving custody of Emily, the further she seemed to pull away. "Hey," he called as he wandered into the kitchen squeezing the keys in his pocket. She looked up from a pot of spaghetti. Emily was in her high chair munching on crackers.

"Hi there." Claire smiled at him then looked away, pushing her long, feathered bangs behind one ear.

"The first coat of paint is finished on the back and sides of the house. We just have the front and the porch to paint—after you take down the gazebo, if you're still going to do it."

Claire nodded her approval. "It won't be too much work, I hope, to reshape the porch on that end so it has a corner instead of a curve after I get someone else to take the gazebo down."

Bradley sighed. "Nothing a circular saw and some nails can't handle."

"Good," Claire mused. "At least the outside of the house will be finished like we planned."

He didn't remind her it was as she'd planned it. She knew he thought taking down the gazebo was a travesty. "All perfect and balanced, just like you want it."

"Nothing off-kilter," she murmured. She scooped up a lump of saucy red noodles and watched them flip back off the ladle into the pot. Before Bradley could remind her again that not everything in life had to be perfectly straightforward, she asked, "Would you like to stay for dinner?" She aimed her chin toward Emily. "Tell Daddy you want him to stay for dinner." Then Claire turned back to Bradley. "Maybe she'll make less of a mess. Spaghetti in this new kitchen freaks me out."

Rather than laugh, Bradley's heart skipped a beat. He'd offered to run out and grab carryout a few times, but Claire seemed to prefer eating at home under the high ceilings in the kitchen. She'd never asked him to stay before, and he'd assumed she wanted her quiet time with the house and Emily. He glanced up at the painted beadboard they'd agreed on since he couldn't talk her into tin tiles on the ceiling. "I'd love to," he admitted, feeling his throat tighten. "It's not like I have anything better at the loft."

He couldn't bring himself to say "home." The loft had never felt like a home. His studio apartment above the pharmacy was not a sanctuary, not like this. Maybe it would feel like one when Emily came to stay. The thought of that made him breathless with anxiety—and fear. How could he possibly raise a little girl on his own?

"It won't be easy," allowed Claire, moving over to the freshly resurfaced white cabinets. She pulled a door open and withdrew two glass plates and a plastic bowl.

"Are you reading my mind?" Bradley tossed his keys on the new glittery quartz countertop by the back door and slumped into a chair at the table. He pulled the high chair close to be nearer to Emily.

"If you mean keeping Emily fed, then yes. She eats more than I do."

"Eat," Emily agreed.

Bradley chuckled and brushed the toddler's growing locks out of her brown eyes. "Actually, I think as we work out a schedule, it may be better for her to eat over here, if you don't mind?"

Claire fell quiet for a moment then said, "I guess it'll depend what time I finish with work."

"Oh, right. You'll be sculpting full-time."

She brought over two plates heaped with pasta and set them on the table. "Hopefully," she admitted, "but I would rearrange anything if Emily needed me. The truth is, I may have to go get a job with all of these unexpected expenses. I'd planned to live on a percentage of Miss Henny's gift, but the house has swallowed up more than I expected."

Bradley frowned. "I'm sorry." He tried to think of a solution, but the only idea that popped into his mind was living at Henny House and playing with Emily when he wasn't at a job site, and while she was sleeping he could… He pushed away a mental picture of cuddling with Claire on the threadbare sofa in front of the fireplace. "I'm home in the afternoons and evenings, and I don't have to work weekends," he stammered instead.

Claire passed him a bowl to give to Emily, and he set it on the high chair tray. Once seated across from one another, Claire clasped her hands on the table. Her cheeks looked flushed, and he wondered what she was thinking. She gave a dry laugh and small shake of her head. "I guess I could work evenings if I got a new job."

You wouldn't have to if we were together. The intruding thought didn't surprise Bradley, but he knew it was impossible. He'd known the moment they were dancing around the gazebo with rain falling around them, and he'd wanted to kiss her teasingly on the lips. As if sensing his intentions, Claire had pulled herself from his arms and reached out to rescue Emily. The little girl would always come before her own heart.

Bradley realized with a quiet start that this is what made Claire a wonderful mother. And yet, he wanted her to want him. Not in the way he'd wanted Dori. He felt so much more for Claire, and it burned beyond friendship. Surely that meant he'd be wounded all the more when she couldn't offer the same in return.

Claire reached across the table and Bradley met her eyes in wonder. "Blessing on the food," she reminded him.

"Oh." He chuckled lamely. When they clasped hands,

it felt like a lock clicked shut. Bradley pretended to ignore it and reached for Emily. She was eating spaghetti with her fingers but dropped the noodles and held out her tomato-stained palms.

Claire laughed at his expression of dismay. "Maybe we'll just hold your elbows," she told the little girl, "unless you just have to hold your daddy's hand." She pointed at Bradley.

Emily grinned, an orange mustache stained over her top lip. Her eyes sparkled as she met Bradley's with adoration. "Daddy!" she crowed for the first time.

Bradley's eyes watered just as the doorbell rang. Claire gave Bradley an apologetic smile. "That's probably Ms. Olivia. She left a message she's coming for her gelatin bowl that I still have, and she probably saw your truck in the driveway."

Bradley gave her a knowing smile and prepared himself for an extra guest at their little dinner party.

There was no escaping Vi Ainsworth when she set her mind to something, and she wanted Claire to bring Emily to their weekly Sunday gathering at her house. Diane reminded Claire about it on Friday when she stopped by Alabaster's to drop off a stack of business cards she'd ordered for the Art Walk. Diane asked if she'd called Vi back about her Sunday invitation, and though Claire tried not to shrink, the store owner had known at once she'd been stalling and encouraged her to attend.

Claire had to admit it was a beautiful day for a Sunday drive through the countryside around Kudzu Creek's city limits. She and Emily passed several homes on large lots, a long line of black fences, a horse farm, a big barn with a colorful quilt painted on its top door and some cows in a field that excited Emily to the point of speechlessness. The Ainsworths lived along a road off the main highway in a sprawling community with enormous, beautiful lawns and small, rippling meadows beyond them.

It just feels so personal, Claire thought as she pulled into the round driveway of a stucco home, *to attend someone else's family dinner.* They weren't her family, they were Emily's, but both Bradley and Vi had insisted she attend, too, and not just drop Emily off.

Twin columns braced a portico over a black front door and made Claire think of Jefferson's Monticello. The flowerbeds were covered with pink and light yellow rose bushes. "That!" Emily pointed at the house with interest from her car seat.

"That's right," Claire agreed, turning off the ignition. "This is your great-aunt's and uncle's house," she told her. "Vi," Claire reminded her, and Emily parroted, "Vi."

Claire climbed out of the car and unbuckled Emily. Before they reached the front door, it yawned wide and Vi trotted out with her arms held open for hugs. "I knew I'd catch you at church." She grinned.

"Bradley insisted we sit with him." Claire hoped Vi didn't think too much of it. They all knew the history here. Emily was Dori's, and Bradley was Dori's, too. When Vi had cornered her to keep her from fleeing after church on Sunday, Claire had known she should have answered the two messages about dinner left on her phone. "I didn't want to put you out or interfere in your family time."

"Oh, nonsense." Vi flapped a hand at Claire like

she was being a goose. "You're from Kudzu Creek, so you're family. You're always welcome here for dinner."

Emily held her hands out, and Vi took her into her arms with a giant squeeze. "Oh, sweet girl, Auntie Vi is so happy to see you." She grinned at Claire mischievously over Emily's shoulder. "And you, too. I hope you don't mind meatloaf."

"I love it," Claire assured her. "Miss Henny always made the best meatloaf."

"Is that so?"

They walked side-by-side into the house. "Yes, she taught me to cook," Claire explained. "Thank goodness, too."

"Then I should have let you bring a dessert, after all." Vi winked. "I just didn't want to put *you* out."

With a small chuckle, Claire looked with admiration around the open floor plan of Vi's home. A giant sectional couch sat in front of a dormant fireplace with a rock chimney that went all the way to the ceiling. A gourmet kitchen was to the right, along with the dining area overlooking the front windows.

Harold, Vi's husband, whom Claire had met at church, was in the kitchen juggling salt and pepper shakers. Two men seated on barstools at a kitchen island turned around. Bradley jumped up to greet her while his companion leaned back and rested an arm along the island. "You found it! How was Emily's nap?"

"Short." Claire grinned. "But it gave us time to pick up toys and sweep before we get too busy this week."

Emily pointed. "Daddy?"

Vi gasped with delight and passed the baby over into Bradley's arms. "She already knows your name. That's so sweet." She scooted around the island, dodging her husband. Claire watched Emily fling her arms around Bradley's neck. He kissed her on the forehead then looked back over his shoulder toward the man on the barstool.

"Donovan, this is Claire." He raised Emily into the air. "This is Emily."

Donovan, the mysterious cousin who called Bradley's phone at least once a day, slid off the stool and offered Claire a handshake. His dark hair was cropped but, unlike Bradley's, riddled with tight curls. "I've heard a lot about you, seen you around."

"Oh?" She smiled and shook his hand. He was a nice-looking man, more built than his cousin, with wide shoulders and a square face. She'd call him dashing but for the tight curls in his hair; they made him look adorable and innocent.

"Donovan Ainsworth," he said, squeezing her hand.

"You're a lawyer," she remembered, thinking he looked the part.

"That I am," he remarked as if it were no big deal. Vi beamed from across the island counter. "He has his own practice in Kudzu Creek now."

"I heard about that."

"Yes, if you're ever hurt in a car accident or on the job…" he began in a droll tone, and Claire laughed.

Vi clapped. "Come on now, everyone."

Bradley's Uncle Harold was already seated at the head of a reclaimed barnwood table. Its glossy topcoat complimented a dozen soft, covered chairs in different colors of chic upholstery. Bradley hitched Emily onto his hip and touched Claire on the elbow. "Let's eat," he whispered. She realized he was excited to have Emily there and didn't seem to mind she'd come, too. He led her to a seat across the table from his cousin and pulled it out for her, making Harold jump up to scoot out his wife's chair.

"You're making me look bad," his uncle grumbled, and everyone chuckled.

After a prayer, they dug into hot meatloaf with a sweet sauce on top, mashed potatoes and brown gravy, salad and corn on the cob. It was a feast. A family feast. And Claire couldn't help but feel honored to be included. Across the table, Bradley held Emily on his lap and shared his plate with her.

"So, Claire," prompted Donovan from beside Bradley, "I understand you're the new artist in town?"

Relieved she wasn't going to be quizzed about Emily, Claire relaxed. She stirred her fork through her potatoes to cool them off. "Yes, if you want to call it that," she answered modestly. "I'm a ceramist."

Vi pointed to the center of the table. "She makes these amazing oil cruets. Do you remember I bought that from Alabaster's for my homemade dressing? It's perfect."

Claire blushed. She'd recognized it while drizzling her salad with vinaigrette.

"Yes, I know," joked Donovan. "You tell me every time I use it." He shifted his gaze back to Claire. "So how did you know Dori?"

Claire tried not to feel uncomfortable and assumed examining questions were a part of his nature. "We were roommates in our first year in college."

"A long time, then."

"Yes."

"I knew Dori," he said. "I met her a couple times. Nice girl."

"Yes, thank you," Claire replied. She watched him look sideways at Emily. To her surprise, he added, "I'm glad you're here." Speechless, Claire thanked him with a silent nod.

"Now, Bradley…" Aunt Vi pulled their attention back to her side of the table. She gave him a serious look with lips slightly turned down. "Your mother called yesterday, and she didn't say anything about Emily."

An awkward silence fell across the table. Claire watched Bradley turn three shades of pink that ended in fuchsia. She also noticed he wouldn't meet her eyes. "Yes…well, I haven't talked to them in a while so…"

"Not since you started the Henny House project, was it?" prompted Uncle Harold before guiding a fork of meatloaf to his mouth.

"Since they came to dinner here a while back." Bradley cleared his throat. As if sensing his discomfort, Emily twisted around in his lap and stuck a radish slice into his mouth. He gave her an exaggerated smile and chewed. She giggled.

"Bradley." Aunt Vi's tone sounded like she was scolding him now. "Your parents are happy you're back in Georgia, and they liked Dori regardless of what happened. I don't think it's fair to keep Emily from them, especially if we know."

"All of Kudzu Creek knows," agreed Donovan.

Bradley darted a perturbed glance his way, and his cousin winced.

"I'm going to," Bradley promised, "when the time is right. Besides, there are still some court proceedings, and a social worker just contacted me, so I have those to deal with. We have a ways to go."

"I'll help you," Claire volunteered before she could stop herself.

He looked up with gratitude. She couldn't imagine why he hadn't yet told his parents he had a daughter. It was clear he loved Emily and was proud of her.

Harold changed the conversation by asking Donovan about his last case, which he summarized with wry humor. The talk then turned to Harold's golf statistics and dessert.

"Let me help." Claire jumped up to accompany Vi when she rose to take a platter to the kitchen.

"No, no, you just sit tight. I'm sure the boys will let you help with dishes."

"You can take my spot," Donovan volunteered.

Bradley laughed and caught her eye. "We'll give Uncle Don babysitting duty, and you and I can wash together."

"Okay." Claire didn't mind at all, and after everyone helped clear the table after the key lime pie was consumed, she hurried to the sink to get started. She wanted to do her part; after all, the dinner had been wonderful. Donovan claimed an allergy to holding babies, and Aunt Vi asked if she could take Emily outside to see the dogs. Her gaze bounced back and forth between Claire and Bradley.

Claire held her breath and waited. She knew she would have to let go at some point. Feeling Bradley's questioning stare, she squeezed her hands and remained silent.

"I… I guess that's okay," he spluttered.

"Blow Daddy a kiss." Vi encouraged Emily, who did so with impatience.

"Pony!" she begged and, laughing, the older couple took her outside.

"I'm going to head out back to the guesthouse for a nap," Donovan announced. He picked up a piece of leftover crust from the breadbasket on the island. "It was nice to meet you finally," he told Claire, and she nodded. Standing behind the dishes in the sink, she felt more comfortable. She turned on the tap and let the water run. "You, too. Thanks for letting me crash your Sunday dinner."

He cocked his head at her. "You didn't crash anything. You're practically family." His kind reassurance warmed her heart, and she couldn't help but smile at his sincere look.

Bradley came up beside her and dropped a stack of plates into the wide farm sink. "I'll see you tomorrow," he told his cousin.

"Lunch at Kudzu's after my case?"

Bradley gave a slight nod. "I'll text you when I get to a stopping point."

As Donovan disappeared through a sliding-glass door beside the fireplace, the house seemed to settle. Except for the streaming water and clattering dishes, it felt peaceful and quiet. Claire and Bradley worked in tandem; she rinsed, and he loaded the dishwasher. As the last of the silverware went in, Claire squeezed the water from a sponge and started on the counters.

"You're a hard worker."

"I am when you feed me," Claire joked. She was so used to being around Bradley, this didn't feel any different. It was just another house.

"They like you, but you knew that."

This pleased Claire.

"Did you ever call Miss Henny 'mom'?" Bradley scooted up onto the damp counter she'd just cleaned.

Claire shook her head. "No. As a matter of fact, I never considered her my mother until lately. I'd never thought of anyone that way."

He wrinkled his forehead. "I wonder why you're just now giving yourself permission."

Claire concentrated on finding stray crumbs on the marble surface. "It's not conscious," she mumbled. The sponge in her hand stopped moving. "You know what?" She turned to meet Bradley's gaze. "I don't think I ever thought of Henny House as my own house back then either. I knew it was a place I loved and where I felt welcome, but living here again and fixing things up, I've started thinking about it in a different way. Not as just a house but as my home."

"Of course it's your home, silly," Bradley teased. "You're family, like Donovan said."

Claire smiled. "I was lucky to have Miss Henny. Between meeting Dori and Emily, and now you, it sometimes seems like too much to ask for."

"Dori," breathed out Bradley. "Right." He slid off the counter and leaned against it, folding his arms snugly against his chest. Something flickered in his beautiful mossy-brown eyes.

Claire tossed the sponge in the sink. "Okay, then." She took a deep breath. It was time to close the wound he couldn't seem to leave alone every time Dori's name was brought up. "Dori was scared. You do know she was putting off going to med school. Her parents were pressing her to become a doctor, but her heart wasn't in it."

Bradley lifted his chin to show he knew that much.

"That's one of the reasons why she moved to California with you," Claire continued.

"You mean ran." Bradley corrected her in a low voice. "We were tired of our parents making our decisions."

Claire grimaced. "I knew she'd gone out there with you because we emailed off and on. Then one day she called. She wanted to come home. Not Georgia, but back to Birmingham where we'd gone to school. I was working full-time while sculpting on the side, and having a roommate would help make ends meet. So she moved in."

Bradley squeezed his arms. "We signed the annulment papers by fax. A few weeks later, she sent her last email and asked me not to reply. She needed space and time before she felt like we could have any kind of relationship again, but she didn't even hint that she was having a baby."

"She thought it would be best," Claire explained. "The fallout from your families after you eloped was terrible."

"That's because I wasn't good enough since I'd decided not to go into law or accounting like my parents wanted, not to mention I interfered with her parents' dreams of her becoming a doctor." Bradley's tone echoed with frustration. "What did she plan to do next? Be a single mom and never tell me I had a little girl?"

Claire balled her fists, praying she could make Bradley understand so he could find peace. "It wasn't like that. She knew she'd raise Emily alone if she had to, but going through the motions applying to med school again made her parents happy. I told her I'd help because we were like sisters. I never had one, you see." Claire's voice broke. He met her eyes with sympathy.

"Bradley, she was trying to figure out what to do besides medicine, how to be a mother, a divorcee and how long to wait before telling you about Emily. She wanted you to keep the job you'd landed with the historical preservation firm in San Francisco. She loved you that much."

"So it was a sacrifice?" he wondered. "She thought she was sparing me?"

"From any more pain," Claire promised. "She thought you were more upset about splitting up than you admitted."

Bradley's shoulders slumped. "Maybe I was. Or maybe it was my pride. Or maybe it was just failing at something I wanted to prove to everyone I could do—have a career and a wife..."

"It just wasn't the right time," Claire said softly.

He raised his eyes to hers. "I know."

Claire met his gaze with steady determination. She could stare at him for hours. Not just talk—but gaze into his face and get lost. There was something about being with him that made her feel at peace and—though she hesitated to admit it—complete. Balanced, even though it wasn't perfect. Her mind flitted to the gazebo she had yet to disassemble.

"Claire," Bradley said in a quiet tone, "I know you never felt you had a true home because of the circumstances you grew up in, but it doesn't mean you can't have one now. Or a family." Bradley's voice sounded deep and throaty. He studied her intently until Claire felt her cheeks do a slow, deep burn. It coursed through her and pooled in her heart like simmering lava.

He must have seen it happen. Bradley crossed the yawning space between them in two steps. "If you believe Dori wanted me to be happy, then you have to believe she'd want you to be happy, too. I'm glad you love it here, Claire. I do, too. And I'm happy you like Aunt Vi. She loves you. We all do, and we're here for you. I'm here for you. For anything you need. I want you to be happy. I want..."

Claire would have smiled at the compliment, but Bradley was staring into her eyes as if trying to send her a message. What more could he do for her? "You've already promised to share Emily with me," she began with a nervous breath. "I don't know what else I could ask for." She knew it was an enormous white lie when she uttered it. Dori would have laughed.

"You don't?" Bradley whispered back.

Claire tried to read the meaning in his words and the message in his gaze, but she couldn't allow herself to believe what she saw there even if Dori would have approved. If she was wrong, or when life pulled out the rug from under her again, she would be alone once more and might even lose Emily this time.

Panic seized her thumping heart. It hungered for him, Claire realized. Did he know? Did he feel the same way? She looked up through her lashes into his eyes, confused and frightened at the emotions swirling like dust devils through her.

Bradley bowed his head over hers and touched her lips with his. This time it was not a light brush or a friendly peck on the cheek. Her whole being erupted with hot emotion as her eyelids collapsed against her will. She sank into him, and his hands went around her waist. Softly, he covered her mouth with his in a kiss that made her squeeze his arms until her fingers ached as much as her heart.

Chapter Ten

It rained Friday, but Saturday morning dawned bright and clear. Bradley sighed with relief and gratitude for Claire's sake. She had high hopes her pottery would be a hit at the Art Walk so she could get her business moving forward, even if it had just begun in a little shed in her backyard.

"Come in!" she called when he rapped on the door. When he walked into Henny House, she was dashing back and forth between Emily's wants and packing a plastic tote of supplies she needed to drive over to Alabaster's.

Bradley's heart jumped at the sight of Claire, and the now-familiar emotion amazed him. He saw her almost every day, but the first moment he laid eyes on her and her gaze sparkled back still got to him. Over the past week, he'd done nothing more than peck her on the cheek when he left for the loft, but he was only holding back until he thought she was really ready—that she believed in the growing feelings he harbored for her. She seemed to accept their attraction to one another, but he could tell she still had doubts that she fit into his life.

She'd left in search of Emily after their moment in Aunt Vi's kitchen exploring their feelings the previous Sunday, but she'd given in to his aunt's insistence she stay for a round of board games. They'd played until Emily grew grumpy and then Claire had abruptly taken her home. The next day, it was hard not to grin at Claire's initial blush when he'd greeted her, but it hadn't taken long for the shy anxiety between them to return to discussions about the house or Emily's schedule.

"Daddy!" Emily shrieked when she heard his footsteps. She darted out of the master bedroom she shared with Claire in thick white potty-training pants and threw herself around his leg.

He laughed. "Good morning, Sunshine."

From the other end of the hall, Claire stuck her head around the kitchen door. "More like Super Nova," she jested. "She's running a hundred miles an hour this morning."

"Is there anything I can help you with before I pack her in the stroller?"

Claire pushed up the elbow-length sleeves on a white blouse that had little sunflowers printed on it. "No, I think I have everything ready. Thank you for taking her to the festival for me. It's one less thing."

"Of course." Bradley raised his brows for emphasis. "This is a big day. Everyone's heard about your work, and people want to see more of it for themselves." Claire smiled hopefully. "Just let me run up and check on the final touchups on the bathroom," Bradley said. "Are you happy with it?"

She nodded. "The bathroom is great. Thanks for making sure it was done right. Not that I ever use the rooms upstairs, but getting them done gives me some peace of mind since I don't know how things will go in the future."

He smiled, resisting the urge to cross the space between them and embrace her. Instead, he lifted Emily and bounced her up and down in his arms. "You're going to do fine. It's a big step, but if I can quit a master's program, drive across the country with no place to live and bungle my way through construction jobs into becoming a historical preservationist, you can sustain yourself as an artist."

A smile tweaked her cheek. "You had Dori."

He studied her. "You have me."

A smile hovered over Claire's face, and he saw her shoulders relax. "Well, thank you, Brad Bo Ainsworth. I really don't want to go back to dealing with department-store customers right now."

"No worries." He grinned. "You own this house, and at the most, another job would be part-time, right? Isn't that what you calculated? So don't worry. Now, I'm going to get this little girl dressed appropriately."

Claire pointed past him. "The diaper bag is packed in her room, the stroller is on the back porch, and don't forget her sunscreen," she admonished him. "I'm heading off, okay?"

"Sure," he encouraged her. "Have fun. I hope you meet lots of new people today."

Claire winced and smiled at the same time to show her anxiety. "Thanks!"

Bradley heard the back door open as he carried Emily down the hall wondering what would have happened if he'd had the courage to kiss Claire goodbye. He'd fought the urge all week long. Just brushing against her filled him with electric elation, but he couldn't bring himself to corner her again. Vi had already given her stamp of approval, and it pleased him, but more importantly, how did Claire feel about him, when Emily was what mattered most?

Emily smelled like syrup, and Bradley kissed her cheek and inhaled her sweetness. Her adoring look of devotion made his heart melt. To think that Emily trusted him and that he could love her forever nearly made him cry. How had he lived almost thirty-two years without feeling such unconditional love? She was the greatest thing Dori had ever done for him. He forgave her, he realized. What was done was done, and she had loved him enough to bring a daughter into the world.

After buckling tiny pink sandals onto Emily's feet that made his fingers feel clumsy, Bradley loaded up the stroller, strapped her inside with a glittery toddler-size ball cap and set off. He felt a surge of pride walking with his daughter after he waved at Mr. Thu as they started down the sidewalk. The Art Walk started early to beat the heat and humidity Kudzu Creek had to endure the majority of the year, and he wanted to visit before the day got too hot.

"I mean to head that way in a bit," called Mr. Thu after Bradley pointed downtown. "Give Claire my best."

"Will do!" Bradley returned. Mr. Thu resumed trimming the grass along his house's foundation. Emily sang a nursery rhyme about bananas at the top of her lungs. The occasional neighbor stopped and stared, as if wondering where Claire had gone. Now it was all Bradley, with a diaper bag and snacks at the ready. He sang along with Emily and listened to their voices echo off the houses in the neighborhood.

The Art Walk included almost every store in downtown Kudzu. Even if the proprietors didn't sponsor a local artisan or craftsperson, employees stood outside with business cards and treats to hand out. Bradley had the strange feeling he was trick-or-treating as he stopped at the hair salon on the corner. One of the hairdressers gave Emily a sucker.

Crossing the street, her loot began to increase as Bradley talked with neighbors about the repairs on Henny House and confirmed rumors that it would be painted in the front after Claire had the gazebo removed Some expressed surprise at the changes. Others didn't seem to mind seeing the dilapidated gazebo go.

He found his boss standing outside Parker and Associates with his wife and a few staff members. Bradley stopped at their table and admired some framed blueprints and photographs of homes that had been built or refurbished. His Monroe project was featured.

"Is this your little girl we've heard so much about?" Mr. Parker leaned forward and gave Emily a silly grin. She giggled and shied away from him. Mrs. Parker held out a small bag of fruit snacks. "May I?"

It seemed all of Kudzu Creek knew about Emily now. Bradley squeezed the stroller's handlebar. He really needed to call his parents. They needed to have a long talk. His heart did a nervous somersault at the prospect, but Bradley smiled. "She'd love that."

She presented it to Emily, and the baby's mouth dropped in awe. "Snacks!" she crowed with delight and squished the bag.

Bradley chuckled. "Yes, this is Emily. Her mother passed away a few months after she was born."

"You've made a good decision raising her in Kudzu Creek," his boss said approvingly.

"I think so, too," agreed Bradley.

"Daddy!" Emily pleaded, holding up the snack bag she couldn't open.

"I better move along." Bradley opened the snack bag, waved goodbye and coaxed Emily to thank the couple for her treat. They rolled on until he reached a crowd in the middle of the sidewalk. At first, he thought it was a line for Kudzu's, but the mob filled the entire area around the front of Alabaster's, and he realized it was for the gift shop.

Ms. Olivia wandered past and held up an oil cruet. "Look what I found," she crowed.

"You'll love it. My aunt sure does."

Ms. Olivia smiled and gave him a small wave. "I have to meet the pastor at the Peachtree Market. We're going to buy day-old bread for the food pantry."

Bradley told her goodbye and maneuvered the stroller through the crowd until it became impossible. Bored, Emily stuck her fingers out and snatched at knees around her. Her wet hands oozed with squashed fruit snacks. When a man turned with a sharp jerk at her touch, Bradley saw it was Laurel Murphy's husband, Kyle.

"I'm sorry," Bradley apologized as he intervened. He tried not to laugh under his breath.

Kyle wiped the toddler's juicy handprint off his leg. Beside him, Laurel, wearing an orange skirt and low heels, turned around.

"Oh, Mr. Ainsworth," she tutted.

"Bradley," he offered.

She looked down at Emily then met his eyes with a tight, pert smile. "I never heard back from you about the paint sample card. Did Claire give it to you?"

"Yes, she did," Bradley replied, "but she'd already made her decision."

The woman pursed her lips. "I hoped you would change her mind about that, not to mention the gazebo."

Bradley licked his bottom lip. Trying to explain that he would not fight a homeowner over paint was useless, and he'd lost the gazebo battle. It was Claire's decision how much of the past she wanted to preserve. She was a woman who wanted to move on. "She isn't concerned about a historical plaque from the board, but I am pleased she chose an appropriate shade of yellow for the time period. She needs to do what she thinks best for her family."

Laurel's nose wrinkled. "Family? Miss Henny certainly never kept the house up. I'm not surprised some stranger wants to tear half of it down."

"It's just the gazebo," Bradley reminded her, "and Claire isn't a stranger. I advised against it, but she's determined. I assure you the interior of the house is mostly intact."

"Mostly?" Laurel sighed as people whirred around them. "Well, I'm sorry to tell you that you weren't selected for the position on the board. There was a vote, and we chose someone else with less…going on."

Bradley's atmospheric mood crashed to the ground. He didn't miss Laurel's suggestive glance to her husband that was like a finger-point at Emily. A surge of defensiveness raced through him, and he pushed away the disappointment about not being chosen for the board. "If you mean my daughter, I'm more than capable of serving the historical committee and raising a child."

Laurel arched a brow at him and slunk her hand through her husband's arm like she wanted to drag him away. "I'm sorry, but we have to take all things into consideration when we appoint members of the community to positions of leadership." She fanned herself as if the early heat was getting to her. "It's such a disappointment about Henny House."

Bradley clenched his teeth to keep a polite smile pasted on his face. "It's not a disappointment at all. Excuse me." He aimed the stroller toward a narrow alley that led to the backside of Alabaster's and strode away. Emily became overly excited when he parked it behind the shop. She was ready to escape herself.

Smarting at Laurel Murphy's rejection, Bradley tried to wipe Emily's hands and face and not think about how disheartened he felt; how disappointed his family would be. At least his father had seemed impressed he had applied to serve on the board. It would make no difference to Mother, but she'd surely see it as another failure proving her choices of careers for him had been right.

Bradley grunted. Cleaning up Emily was a losing battle, but at least it distracted him from his thoughts. Sugar, food coloring and wetness was smeared all over her. Surrendering to the mess, he decided not to worry about his clean T-shirt. Like him, it would wash.

Unbuckled and packed on the side of his hip, Emily cruised with Bradley through the crowd to check out the windows of Alabaster's. She delighted in everything shiny around them. In the window, some of Claire's colorful pottery was showcased on top of an ivory drop cloth along with decorative strings of beads and small framed mirrors. One vintage-inspired lemonade pitcher spun slowly on a rotating stand.

Elbows bumped him in the back, and Bradley maneuvered Emily around to show her Claire's work. "See? Claire's bowls?"

Emily spat out a fruit snack and it slid down her chin, leaving a red trail of drool. She pointed at the window just as he caught the mess from her mouth in his hand. For a split second, the gooeyness made him want to sling it to the ground and wipe his hands on his pants, but the hilarity of the moment made him chuckle. He held on to the half-eaten fruit gummy to push back into her mouth the next time she belted out, "Snacks!"

With his little girl held to his chest with one arm, Bradley mingled with the crowd spilling in and out of Alabaster's front door. There were two tables in front of the store. At one, a silversmith had jewelry spread out. Bradley found Claire and Diane at the other table with pieces of Claire's collection displayed on a solid black tablecloth. Each one had a description and a price. On the corner of the table sat Claire's business cards and a stack of flyers about Alabaster's.

"Well, hello there," cried Diane.

Emily clapped her hands. "Hi," she chirped, and Bradley thought she looked adorable even with red drool staining her chin. He looked for her foster mom—her mother—and found Claire radiant. She was smiling, chatting and leaning out of her seat to shake hands with people who asked questions about her work. It seemed like the whole world was exploring Alabaster's. When he finally caught Claire's eye, he beamed at her, and she grinned. Then someone picked up one of her pieces ignoring the Do Not Touch sign and handed her a credit card. She turned to tend to her new customer.

"Are you going to buy something?"

Bradley looked to find Donovan beside him. Emily

recognized him and pointed with a sticky finger. His cousin jumped back. He gulped. "Whoa, there."

Bradley laughed. "Still allergic?"

"Only if they're covered in goo." Donovan ran his fingers through his tight curls as if the toddler had mussed them. He looked more casual in khaki shorts and a golf shirt than his usual slacks and tie. "Mom said to pick up another cruet to keep on the kitchen island. She needs two, evidently."

"That's not a bad idea with as much salad as she eats," Bradley mused. "There are pieces in the window over there, too."

"It looks like Claire's doing well."

"It's a good start." Bradley hiked Emily up higher so she could see Claire. The little girl began to squirm, and he dropped the fruit snack from his hand to catch her.

"I must say you're handling fatherhood well," Donovan teased. "But what was that in your fist?" Before Bradley could retort or offer him a fruit snack, Donovan strode forward and shook Claire's hand while she was free again. Bradley edged up beside him at the table.

"Down!" insisted Emily when she saw Claire.

"How are you?" Claire asked Donovan cheerily. "No cases today?"

"Not on the weekend, thank goodness. I'm just picking up something for my mom."

"Vi?" Claire sighed. "She's so sweet. She already has something."

"Apparently she finds your things useful." Donovan scanned the table display with interest. "I'll take one of your business cards for myself. I have a friend who is setting up a law office in Albany, and he asked me if I knew any decorators. I told him about your work."

"Sure!" Claire handed him a card. "I really appreciate that, Donovan." He smiled and began to peruse the table.

"Ca-re!" Emily cried.

Claire curled her fingers in a little wave. "It's okay, Emily. You stay with Daddy."

"Ca-re," the little girl insisted. She twisted and kicked her legs, so Bradley set her on the ground but kept hold of her hand. "She's so sticky, I think we'll be cemented together," he joked.

"I see that." Claire pointed to his chest and Bradley looked down. His T-shirt was stained with a rainbow of colorful, sugary, baby saliva strings. He groaned and swiped at them, and they spread around like watercolors. Claire snickered. "Just wait until she gets a hold of one of Mac's fruit tarts." She motioned toward Kudzu's.

"No thanks, I've seen her with spaghetti."

Claire threw her head back and laughed, and beside her, Diane pointed at him. "You serve it, you clean it up," she admonished him.

"I thought fruit snacks would be harmless," Bradley complained. "Her mama could have warned me."

Claire gave a sheepish chuckle that turned down her mouth. "Technically, I'm not her mother."

Bradley's stomach sank. How had that slipped out? The daydreams skipping around in the back of his head were sneaking their way out.

Donovan saved him by edging over to Claire and handing her a cruet. "I'll take this one, please. Can you wrap it really well for me, and I'll go inside and look at the lemonade pitcher for my friend."

"I'd be happy to." Claire rearranged a smile on her

face and reached for some tissue while Diane took Donovan's credit card.

Emily backed into Bradley's legs with a smack, and he looked down to make sure she hadn't tripped. She was shying away from a woman crouched too close to her on the ground. Bradley's mood took another dive when he noticed his father a step away, a frown on his thin face. His thick white hair was clipped shorter than usual over his sunburned forehead, making him look like Uncle Harold.

The familiar woman stood, and her jaw tightened beneath her green eyes. "So I presume this is my granddaughter," she said in an accusing tone that shamed Bradley to the core. His mind raced like a rabbit fleeing from hounds, but he forced himself to speak rather than miss a beat.

"Hello, Mother."

Claire almost dropped the cruet she was wrapping up. Unable to tear her eyes away from the woman Bradley had called "mother," she fumbled to get the gift into the bag then passed it to Donovan, who was watching the scene unfold with round eyes. He sent Claire a small grimace and backed away. It took her a moment to process that he had muttered, "Goodbye and good luck," and she suddenly wished Vi had appeared instead of her son.

A woman in a ponytail asked about a fruit bowl on the other end of the table. Sensing the tension, Diane interceded on Claire's behalf.

"When were you going to tell us?" the woman next to Bradley demanded.

"Soon." Bradley's tone sounded clipped. "We can

talk about it later. I'm taking her home for a nap in a few minutes." He glanced back at Claire helplessly.

"In that cubbyhole over the drugstore?" His mother put her hands on her hips. "Let me see this child of yours, and let's go talk. Now."

Bradley cupped his hand over the top of Emily's head. "Now isn't the time."

"When would be a good time, Brad Bo?" Bradley's father, Claire assumed, finally intervened. She tried to think of something to say, to throw Bradley a lifeline, but her mind was cluttered with what-nows and what-ifs and should-haves and could-haves. Why had Bradley waited so long to tell his parents? How could he be proud enough of Emily to carry her around town but too ashamed to tell his own mother and father?

Bradley shot Claire a look of dread. She'd never seen him so disconcerted before. "I can take a break," she said. "Diane," she interrupted, "would you mind?"

"Of course not." Diane looked at the Ainsworths curiously.

Mrs. Ainsworth swiveled her frown to Claire, her forehead wrinkling as she tried to fit the pieces of the puzzle together.

Bradley intervened. "Mother, Dad, this is Claire Woodbury. She's Emily's guardian."

Claire offered her hand and looked Mrs. Ainsworth in the eye. The woman wavered before accepting it only long enough to touch fingers. "You had guardianship of my granddaughter and didn't think to contact me?"

Claire tried not to notice interested customers stepping back to either watch or walk away from the tense conversation. "I was Dori's best friend," she explained, and both of the grandparents flinched. If they hadn't known Dori was Emily's mother, they did now. "I didn't know for certain who Emily's father was before I came to Kudzu Creek." Mrs. Ainsworth gave her a look of disbelief. "I mean…" Claire faltered. "I had a name and knew that he was from this area, but Dori didn't want to disrupt anyone's lives until she sorted things out."

"I highly doubt that," said Mrs. Ainsworth tersely. "She didn't mind disrupting ours when she talked Bradley into quitting school and running off to California."

"That was my decision, Mother," Bradley reminded her in a raised voice. His cheeks glowed with color.

"You never wanted to be a construction worker," she sniped.

"Actually I did. I loved it. *You* didn't want me to be one," Bradley replied. "And by the way, that isn't exactly what I do, not that it matters. It's honest and respectable work for anyone."

Heat poured from the sunny sky, toasting Claire's head and making her feel light-headed.

Mr. Ainsworth cleared his throat and looked around. "Now, Cici, I think we should talk about this somewhere else. Your apartment?" he asked Bradley pointedly.

Bradley's jaw twitched. "It's too small, and Emily needs her nap." He glanced at Claire with a question in his eyes, and she nodded her approval. "You can meet us at Henny House," she told his parents. "It's the Victorian on Maple Grove Lane, around the corner."

Bradley gave them the address.

Mr. Ainsworth eyed Kudzu's next door. "I'm going to grab something to drink first, and we'll be right along," he promised in a calm tone.

"No. Now," his wife insisted. "It's bad enough I had to hear about this from someone I hardly knew."

"Where did you hear it from?" queried Bradley.

She surprised Claire when she didn't blame his cousin. "From my next-door neighbor, who teaches piano lessons to the grand-niece of one of your neighbors."

"Mr. Thu?" Bradley asked in confusion.

"No," his mother snapped, "a woman named Olivia Cleveland, whom I intend to meet and thank today."

It was all too much for Emily. She held her arms up to Bradley. "Daddy," she whined.

Claire resisted the urge to push everyone out of the way and scoop her up. "You're upsetting the baby," she told them all in a stiff tone. "We'll meet you at Henny House in a half hour." She raised her chin at Mr. Ainsworth. "Parker and Associates has a booth set up down there. Why don't you take a few minutes and see what Bradley does before coming by? It'll give me time to make arrangements with my inventory here."

Mrs. Ainsworth scowled at Claire's suggestion.

"Daddy!" Emily screeched.

"That's a good idea," Bradley agreed. "I'll see you both at Henny House."

A short pause filled with tension whirled between them. "Fine," retorted Mrs. Ainsworth. She crouched again in front of Emily. "Grandmama will see you in a little bit, Emmy."

Claire's mouth soured. Emily spit out a lump of something dreadful that looked like a chewed fruit snack. It hit the street with a plop. "No," she grumbled like she did when she was tired.

Mrs. Ainsworth reared back. "My goodness, she's a mess," she scolded. She stomped to her feet and gave

Bradley's dirty T-shirt a searing look of disapproval. "And so are you!"

"Mrs. Ainsworth," blurted Claire, feeling her temper ready to bypass her common sense. Reacting in anger was the one thing Miss Henny had preached to never allow. "We will see you in a little bit, but for now, please excuse us."

The look of offense the woman shot her was loaded with needles, but Claire only felt them for a moment because, from the side of her eye, she saw Emily dart away. Before she could warn Bradley, he reached out, but Emily dodged him and grabbed a handful of black tablecloth along the way. She ran off with a giggle, daring him to chase her.

Claire watched in slow motion as her pottery began to slide along the table. She opened her mouth to cry out, but it stuck in her throat. Diane jumped back in surprise, and the ceramic pieces toppled like dominoes and crashed onto the ground. The explosive sound of fired clay splintering on the pavement was like being shot in the heart. There were a few audible gasps, and everyone outside Alabaster's stopped speaking at once and stared.

Claire grabbed her stomach to keep from dropping to her knees in a faint of horror. What happened next she wasn't sure, because she had to walk away, trusting Bradley would collect Emily, and Diane would take care of the disaster spread around the table.

With a bolt, Claire's legs flew down the sidewalk as she tried to think, but all she could do was feel, and it was an awful sensation. Her work destroyed. Her baby taken. And Bradley? Her feelings for him had sparked hope and secret fantasies that had begun the first moment he'd stepped into her life—into Henny House—she admitted. But his parents' disapproval of her was clear.

Claire forced herself not to sob, straightened her spine and hurried down the sidewalk, avoiding eye contact with anyone in her way. She made it past Parker and Associates and the remaining storefronts to the crosswalk without crumpling but fairly leaped into the street. A car horn blared, and the sound jolted her so hard her knees buckled. She stumbled, thinking she would fall, but two strong arms went around her waist and carried her the rest of the way across the street to the other side.

"What are you doing? You were almost run over!" Bradley looked exasperated as he set her down on her feet. His arms stayed around her, and she fought the instinct to throw her clenched fists against his chest and pound him with blame.

"Claire, I'm sorry about your table. I'll pay for the pottery. All of it."

Charity? She didn't want a good deed. She wanted to be a successful artist, her little girl and… Claire forced herself to snap out of it. "No," she squeaked.

Bradley took her by the chin and made her look him in the face. "Diane has Emily. My mother and father went into Kudzu's to get some lunch." He dropped his hand and embraced her again, snugly, so she couldn't escape. Miserable, she didn't want to, but she knew she was prolonging the inevitable.

My life is falling apart. "My things are—"

"Donovan is sweeping up," Bradley said. "Diane called Aunt Vi to come pick up Emily, and she'll take care of everything else. You still have your pottery in the window." He brushed a kiss across Claire's ear, and it tingled, although she tried to ignore it. He couldn't fix this. She wasn't a house, and she had no history. No roots. She'd just have to do what she'd always done and pull herself up by her bootstraps and begin again. *Life story.*

Claire leaned into Bradley's chest and sniffled. His cotton T-shirt felt like glue, and she remembered Emily had gotten him sticky. She pulled away and wiped goo off her cheek with the back of her wrist.

"Oh, I'm sorry," Bradley whispered, but a small laugh spurted out along with the apology. "It's…here." He rubbed his fingertips across her face, and she relaxed a little, looking into his eyes and seeing everything she wanted in his gaze. He lowered his head like he would kiss her, but she forced herself to turn away. It would just hurt more later when he left and took Emily with him, if that's what his parents wanted. Life was temporary. It always had been. Love was temporary, too. Wasn't it?

"Claire, I'm sorry about this. I—"

"You should have told them."

"My parents? Yes. It's just—"

"You didn't because of Dori and because of me, too. Because we…" Claire stopped. She didn't need to point out he had kissed his daughter's caretaker, and worse, that she clearly had feelings for him.

"That's not true." Bradley gulped. "I wanted to, but they've been disappointed in me ever since I ran off." He shrugged his shoulders. "It wasn't really Dori. It was me not doing what they wanted for me, and we argued constantly. I guess I thought rebelling was the only way to make them see, but I came back to make things right, to make them proud—impress them."

Claire wanted to believe him. "I guess having a little girl isn't something they can be proud of then."

Bradley sucked in a breath that sounded frustrated. "My mother isn't just embarrassed about my career choice. She thinks having a divorced son is humiliating."

"That's terrible." Claire relented.

"I have an older sister in Tampa," Bradley explained. "Theresa did everything by the book, their book, and I didn't."

"No wonder you went to California."

Bradley nodded. "Dori knew everything. She was worried about me going alone, so we drove out together without telling anyone. Then in the excitement of it all, one thing led to another..."

"I know," said Claire. She knew the rest of the story. "So your parents blame Dori because you're a contractor now."

"Yes." Bradley exhaled heavily. "Instead of believing I could make my own choices, they blamed Dori for influencing me. After we split up, they wouldn't even speak her name. I had no idea how I was going to explain Emily to them or why Dori never told anyone. They expect me to be perfect—like your house without the gazebo, perfectly square and balanced—and they blame everyone else for the mistakes *I* make." His voice crackled with emotion.

"They want me to live their version of what they think my life should be, but I can't do that, so I—I put off telling them about Emily because I didn't want another confrontation like before when Dori and I took off."

Claire realized they were drawing attention standing

on the street corner. People would think things, things the Ainsworths wouldn't like. She pulled out of Bradley's arms, but it felt like tearing out a piece of her heart. Explaining that something was going on between them would be even more difficult than explaining Emily and the promise she'd made, she suspected. Worst of all, she was his ex-wife's best friend.

"We should get home," Claire whispered and started down the sidewalk.

A clunking car rolled by at an impossibly low speed, and she looked up in time to see Ms. Olivia's eyes round with curiosity and concern. Claire gave her an abrupt wave instead of stopping her to ask her why she was driving at her age; why she had called her relative in Lake Charles to talk about Emily and Bradley. It would do no good. Claire knew Ms. Olivia meant well; that she thought of everyone she met as family. It wasn't Ms. Olivia's fault that Claire felt like she was going to be sick at this very moment. Everything she'd dreaded had come to pass.

Bradley grabbed her hand. "It's going to be okay," he promised her. "They'll understand once we explain the whole story." He sighed. "They're just not going to be happy."

"They will be," Claire murmured. She slipped her hand out of his and ducked under the extended arm of a low tree branch. "If they love you, they will love Emily." It sounded like something Miss Henny would say, but was it true? The Ainsworths didn't seem like Aunt Vi and Uncle Harold. Would they accept Dori's little girl? If not, they would never accept Claire.

As if reading her mind, Bradley pulled her to a stop

again. "They will, Claire, and they'll love you, too, once I tell them everything you've done for us."

Us. He meant Emily and himself, Claire decided.

"Look…" he stammered, "I care about you. More than you know. We're a part of one another's lives now, but something's happened between us that goes far beyond sharing Emily. Maybe we could be more."

Claire realized it was time to stop going wherever their hearts were headed before one of them was hurt beyond repair. "I care about you, too, Bradley, but we have to think about other people."

"Dori's gone, Claire," Bradley muttered.

"I know. I've made peace with that, but Emily's here," Claire replied, "and so is your family."

"So?"

She fell silent. How could she explain she knew she would never belong? He might believe he liked her now, but that didn't mean he'd decide one day he didn't see them together for life.

"Claire?" Bradley's voice was pleading. "One moment I think you have feelings for me, real feelings, even passionate ones, but then you shut down like we're just…friends."

Claire's eyes burned. She swallowed so the words didn't choke her. "I have to be realistic, Bradley, and you make me forget that and dream big dreams. The reality is, you're Emily's birth parent, and I will never be. You are her father, and I can only mother her until someone else takes my place. That's what guardians do. Besides, it looks like your mother wants the job." A sob began to work its way up her throat. Bradley paled. Claire inhaled a painful breath that cramped her side. "Bradley, I can't let myself fall into a love I can't fall out of, and that scares me with you. You loved Dori, and I know you feel it was more friendship than true love, but I… Look at me. I have no family, no roots. I could never be anything more than your daughter's friend, her Miss Henny." With a sharp breath, Claire rushed down the sidewalk ahead of him, hoping he didn't follow. "Go spend time with your mother and father," she called. "We can discuss parenting later when they're ready to come over and talk."

"But Claire," he insisted in a voice that sounded desperate, "you're her mother now!"

Claire stumbled up the front steps of Henny House intent on bursting through the door and hurtling herself up the stairs and locking herself in the newly finished bathroom. It would be the perfect place to cry, to let it all out, and no one would be the wiser. The tears she was fighting began to drip, and her jaw ached from clenching her teeth. She rattled the key impatiently in the lock.

"Claire, is something wrong?"

With a surprised jerk, she looked sideways. Mr. Thu stood on the bottom step behind her.

"Is everything okay? I thought the Art Walk had another hour to go."

Almost panting from her run down the street, Claire swiped at her bangs with the useless key in her grip. "Oh, I…" She brushed the wetness off her face. "Emily pulled the tablecloth off my table, and all of the pottery fell onto the ground." She tried to smile like it was no big deal, but it *was* a big deal. The loss of her sales, Emily, Bradley, the Ainsworths…*everything* was a big deal.

Mr. Thu's chiseled face softened, and he climbed the

steps and took her by the elbow. "That's terrible. I'm so sorry." Leaning close to examine her with his dark eyes, he added, "Is there anything I can do?"

She grimaced. "No, what's done is done."

The tender kindness in his gaze made Claire soften. "This is just a hiccup," he assured her. "You had a great day, and there are great days to come."

"You're right." She reached for his hand, resisting the urge to sob on his shoulder like she would have on Miss Henny's. "But that's not all." Her voice faltered. "Bradley's parents were there. They just found out about Emily. It was…uncomfortable."

Mr. Thu looked around the porch. "Why don't you come with me?" He led her by the arm to the gazebo and motioned for her to sit down. "Ms. Olivia told me he was Emily's father, although I suppose I should have figured that one out for myself."

"I hoped she wouldn't say anything and leave it to Bradley to tell."

"We didn't know it was a secret. I'm sure she meant no harm."

"It wasn't a secret." Claire hiccupped. She covered her mouth. "Not anymore, anyway," she said between her fingers. "It wasn't her fault."

"Why don't you sit back and try to calm down," Mr. Thu urged. He reclined beside her, leaning back with his elbows perched behind him.

Claire let out a long steady breath that seemed to empty the tension throbbing in her body. She watched a dog walker stride down the street wrangling three different dogs with great skill and realized she was thankful not to be alone at the moment. A breeze riffled a rosebush in front of the gazebo and tossed up a honeybee. It whizzed over, stopped between Mr. Thu and her, and gave them both a cursory examination before disappearing somewhere up in the rafters.

He chuckled. "I've thought of having some hives in the backyard, but I'm not sure what the neighbors would think."

Claire felt herself unwind. Sitting in the shade, the afternoon felt cozy and calm. "I wouldn't mind," she decided. "Local honey would be great."

"That's true," he agreed. "I wasn't actually thinking of selling it, but it'd be a fun hobby."

She caught herself smiling. "Maybe you could sell it at the Peachtree Market, but are you sure you have time with two yards to keep up?"

"Oh, I don't mind helping you with your grass," he assured her, "and I can't resist the cookies you bring over for compensation. Besides, my yard is so small, and I enjoy seeing Emily."

Claire's heart fell. "I don't know how much longer Emily will live here," she confided. A small sob of despair burst from her mouth. She covered her lips and dabbed her eyes.

Mr. Thu patted her knees. "I sure would miss seeing her, but Bradley will need your help, I suspect, for the time being."

"Yes, he promised me I could still be a part of her life, and from what we've talked about lately, I would keep her during the weekdays. But his parents are here, and I don't know what's going to happen now."

"Maybe it won't be so bad. You'd have time to work in your studio."

"You're right, but I still have to give her up." Claire

wondered if she would ever feel better about it. "I feel like I'm losing her, both of them."

"You mean Bradley."

Claire hadn't meant to divulge so much. She let out a guilty chuckle.

"Ah," said Mr. Thu. "I wouldn't worry about that." He gave her a knowing smile. "I've seen how he looks at you, and it's not all about Emily."

"You think so? I mean..." Claire hesitated. Just because Bradley had kissed her and even hinted he wanted something more didn't mean he wanted to be a permanent part of her life. She wanted a real thing. A family. "I guess I just don't see how it could work out in the long run. Between Emily, her mother's memory and Bradley's parents, I'm not sure how to fit in."

Mr. Thu made a soft noise in his throat. "I thought the same thing when I fell for my wife. She was from Kudzu Creek, and I came from a completely different culture."

Claire listened with interest. "But you made it work?"

"We sure did. Love has a funny way of filling in the gaps we create for ourselves." Mr. Thu looked down the street as if thinking back. "Like with Miss Henny, you know. She lost someone and never wanted to move forward after that, but she was missing something. The kids—you especially, Claire—filled in the gaps. You made Henny House a family home for her until her dying day. I think that's what she wanted for you and that's why she left you this house."

Claire put a hand to her aching throat. "I can never repay her for what she's done, especially now that she's gone."

"But you can," the wise man admonished her, "and

that doesn't mean never having a relationship or children. Those were her choices. She left you the house, not her life decisions."

"Then how?" Claire wondered.

"Live without fear or regrets," Mr. Thu suggested. "You don't need to keep looking back and reliving who you were. You're smart, creative and successful. You're a Henny now. You're from Kudzu Creek." He wrapped an arm around her shoulders, and Claire dropped her head onto it. "You're one of us."

Chapter Eleven

Claire washed her face, ran a comb through her hair and straightened her clothes. The slacks she'd worn to the Art Walk were hot, but she decided not to change into shorts at this point. Even though there were no caseworkers or judges, her first discussion with the Ainsworth family over how to proceed with Emily's life was important. Claire stared at herself in the mirror and thought she looked small and young. The new doorbell Bradley had installed announced he'd arrived with his parents, and she took a deep breath. Miss Henny had done this tens of times and always with grace and wisdom.

Claire floated with trepidation down the hall to the front door. Miss Henny had once told her that, deep down, people only wanted two things: to give love or to be loved, and sometimes the need to be loved manifested itself in ugly ways. Maybe Mrs. Ainsworth had something broken inside that made her the way she was. Her behavior at the Art Walk in front of everyone in town was some kind of cry for help. Claire drew in a breath of courage and pulled open the door.

Bradley stood alongside his father while his mother hung back, looking around the outside of the house. "This hardly looks finished," she mumbled as Claire stepped aside to let them in. Mrs. Ainsworth's observations were cut short when she saw the new chandelier in the foyer hanging over the beautiful floors. She looked impressed.

"You should have seen this place before Bradley and his crew got their hands on it," Claire informed her. "I think most people would have burned it down."

Bradley led the way into the parlor. "I considered it a few times," he joked in an attempt to lighten the mood.

Claire followed them and waited for the older couple to take their seats. The antique furniture had been cleaned and polished so it would make do for another year. It looked rather nice, and a wave of pride washed over Claire. True, it was old-fashioned, compared to what was trendy these days, but the red-velvet sofa and blue-upholstered side chairs made the silvery-gray room look chic and comfortable just like Miss Henny would have liked. A few potted plants had been arranged on the mantel and near the windows. Sheer white curtains allowed sunlight to stream inside, and it bounced off the sheen of the floor in splendid rays.

"What a lovely room," observed Mrs. Ainsworth in a terse voice. Claire slipped into the last empty chair and faced Emily's grandparents. She watched Mrs. Ainsworth study the photos of the toddler over the fireplace. There was one of Dori, too. "So—" the woman began, but her husband interrupted her.

"Bradley tells us you moved here from Birmingham," Mr. Ainsworth prodded. He had blue eyes, and there were deep lines arrowing out from the corners.

"I did," said Claire. "I lived in Henny House from the time I was fourteen until I went to Birmingham. That's where I met Dori."

Mrs. Ainsworth sniffed. "You were a foster child?"

"I didn't know my parents, so yes."

"I see. So you have no family."

The words were bruising. Claire clenched her teeth until it hurt. She had something. She had this house and… Her breath caught in her chest as she looked around the room to avoid frowning at Mrs. Ainsworth. She had her friends and Kudzu Creek.

"Well," soothed Mr. Ainsworth, his tone softer around the edges than his wife's, "that's why we're here. When Cici learned Bradley had a baby, we discussed it and agreed it wouldn't be right to leave our own grandchild in the system."

"It's appalling the Rochesters didn't let us know," Mrs. Ainsworth complained.

"I have to agree with you." Claire thought this helped the tension in the room somewhat. She looked at Bradley and found him sitting ramrod-straight like a soldier with arms crossed over his chest.

"We would like to help with Emily," offered Mr. Ainsworth.

"I told you that's not necessary, Dad," Bradley reminded him. "I can afford to care for Emily myself." His father stared back with a frown but said nothing in return.

"You are a single man, and you've never raised a baby," Mrs. Ainsworth replied in a decided tone.

Watching Bradley's parents gang up on him made Claire ache knowing how humiliating it must feel to be treated like a child. With a soft breath, she turned her attention back to Emily, but Bradley's mother was just getting warmed up.

"We appreciate all you've done for Emily, Claire, but you don't have to worry about her anymore. She's no longer your problem." The woman smiled like she was doing her a favor.

"I'm sorry, what?" Claire shot Bradley a look of concern.

"Now, Mother…" he began.

Without bothering to look his direction, his mother held up her hand to stop him from speaking. Focused on Claire, she continued. "As inconvenient as it is at my age, the Ainsworths do not shirk their responsibilities, so we will take over custodianship of Emily until…well—" she grimaced "—until Bradley gets his life together."

"Mother!"

Claire felt her jaw drop.

"Now, Bradley," his father interjected, "you do have a good job here, and we're impressed with what your boss told us at the festival, but…" He sighed. "Your mother is right. You can't raise a little girl alone."

"He wouldn't be raising her alone," Claire reminded them. "I've had Emily since she was a baby, and I'm the only mother she knows."

"But, dear," returned Mrs. Ainsworth, "you're not a mother." Gently she added, "You didn't have one."

Mr. Thu's words echoed in her mind, and Claire rose to her feet. "Yes, I did," she insisted. "My mother was Glenda Henny. She was the daughter of Elijah Henny, and the great-granddaughter of Dr. Henny, who was the first African American doctor in this town. I thought

I was coming back for Dori, for Emily and my pottery business, but I was coming back home."

Mrs. Ainsworth's eyes rounded like coins, but Claire didn't care. She suddenly felt more like a Henny than anything else. More than a Woodbury. More than a foster child.

Bradley rose and crossed the threadbare Persian rug. He stopped beside Claire's chair. Gazing at his parents, he said in a calm voice, "Claire is a mother, Mother. She's Emily's mother, and I'm Emily's father, and we're going to continue raising her just as we have been."

Claire's heart jettisoned into the air. It was true! She had a family, and she *was* Emily's mother. Dori had made her one. What a gift. Claire clenched her hands.

"You don't even have custody," his mother argued. Sinking back into the sofa, Mr. Ainsworth passed a hand over his face.

"I've been added to the birth certificate," Bradley informed them. "Dori didn't want to do it without my permission."

"Not that she needed it," Mrs. Ainsworth pointed out with a livid glare.

"Even though she was wrong, she wanted to respect what she thought I would want," Bradley retorted. "She always did. Unlike you."

Claire could feel hot, nervous energy radiating from his body as he towered beside her. She inched over closer to him until their arms touched. He was trembling. It seemed having parents didn't always make life perfect for everyone.

At Mrs. Ainsworth's choked silence, Claire took a deep breath. "Dori did the best she knew how, Mrs. Ainsworth, and Bradley is a wonderful father. I know he can do this." She was filled with comfort and courage when Bradley reached for her hand.

"Would you really make your own mother go to court to do what is best for you?" Mrs. Ainsworth's voice sounded hoarse as she locked gazes with her son. "After all we've done for you!" Her eyes flooded with tears.

Claire squeezed his hand to help him be strong. His parents wouldn't have a chance. He squeezed back. "I appreciate all you've done for me. I—I love you, Mom."

Mrs. Ainsworth softened the tiniest bit.

"You know I never wanted to go into accounting, much less law. You knew I wanted to be on the swim team, not the debate team. I did what you wanted me to do for as long as I could bear it. I went to California mostly because of you."

Surprise and hurt flickered across her face.

Bradley took a deep breath. "Growing up means making your own decisions even if it disappoints people. I'm sorry you've never been able to understand that."

"But I do!"

"People don't love you any less because they think differently than you," Claire offered.

Bradley gave a small chuckle to ease the friction. "You should have heard the disagreement we had over remodeling this house." He raised Claire's hand still in his grip. "And we're still friends."

Friends. The words stabbed Claire in the heart. But wasn't that what she'd told Bradley they would have to be? She noticed Mr. Ainsworth's knowing stare and shifted her gaze past her shoulder. It was a terrible mistake to pretend she felt only friendship for him. Bradley was being open and honest with his parents, and she couldn't even admit to herself that she loved him, deeply, and wanted to share everything she'd ever dreamed of with him, not just his daughter. She was letting her past hold her back instead of moving forward like Miss Henny always wanted.

Bradley wasn't finished. "I always knew I wanted to do something different than what you wanted me to do, but that never meant I didn't appreciate or respect you. I'm just sorry it took me until after I graduated high school to be honest about it."

Mrs. Ainsworth's face crumbled, and she covered it with her hands. "Why can't you just be happy and grateful like Theresa?"

Beside Claire, Bradley groaned. Mr. Ainsworth rolled his eyes before he said, "I have no intention of taking my own son to court. We're your parents, not your enemies. We just want what's best for you."

"This is what's best for Emily, and for me," Bradley replied. He sounded stronger, more confident. "Haven't I proved I can do what I set my mind to do? I might have spent more years in college than most people, but I have a degree and a successful career. I'm totally capable of raising Emily."

Claire nodded with encouragement. "He has Aunt Vi and Harold, too."

Mrs. Ainsworth wiped her crocodile tears away, smudging the black eyeliner under her lashes. "But what about us? What do we get to have with Emily? She'll need her grandparents' influence."

"You can come up on weekends or go to church with us," Bradley suggested. "Aunt Vi has given up inviting you to come to Sunday dinners regularly, but I'm sure the offer still stands."

"Weekends?" drawled Mrs. Ainsworth as if it were a paltry sum. Mr. Ainsworth looked like he was about to lose his tee time.

"You could move to Kudzu Creek," Claire reminded them.

"Leave Lake Charles?" Mrs. Ainsworth jerked her head in distaste. "That's impossible. We couldn't uproot our lives and leave. We have all our old friends, and of course the house, which has far more room than this place."

"That's your choice then," Bradley responded, "but if there's anything I've learned, it's not a house that makes a home." He looked at Claire and gave her a small wink.

"Well then." Mr. Ainsworth shifted forward, looked at his watch and clapped his hands together. "Speaking of your aunt and uncle, we have plans with them in a few minutes and would like to spend the evening getting to know Emily with you."

"And talk about this situation a little more," inserted Mrs. Ainsworth, "in private." Clearly the fight wasn't over in her book.

Bradley bobbed his head in an agreeable if not relieved motion. Claire slipped her hand out of his. This was it. She may have been Emily's mother, but it was clear she wasn't going to be accepted as a part of this family and was not wanted at their gathering. Bradley confirmed her feelings when he turned to her. "I'll bring Emily home at bedtime, if that works?"

She put on a brave face. "That'll be fine. It'll give me time to go back to Alabaster's and see about getting my things—the tablecloth at least." She tried not to wither with disappointment. She'd lost hundreds of dollars because of Emily's debacle.

Bradley hugged her, and the warmth of his body against hers made her throat squeeze again. *Friends.*

She fought back tears, willing them to go away. No matter what Mr. Thu had said or how Miss Henny would have advised her, this was about Emily and her father now. Claire would have to let her feelings for Bradley go and leave it to fate—even if fate had rarely been kind.

"I'll see you tonight," he whispered.

She snuck a peek into his eyes and wondered why she couldn't believe what Mr. Thu did. Clearing her throat, Claire followed them to the door. Mrs. Ainsworth stopped in the hall at a black-and-white portrait of Miss Henny with her thick hair coiffed into a beehive hairstyle. "This is Glenda Henny, I presume?" she guessed with a sugary voice coating her repaired emotions.

"Yes. It was taken after she graduated Spelman College with her education degree."

"You seem very different." Mrs. Ainsworth's tone sounded cool.

"Ironic, isn't it?" Claire took a breath. "Because we were almost exactly alike." Peace coursed through her veins and filled her heart. She did belong to Miss Henny. Miss Henny really was her mother, and this house was her home—the Claire Henny house. And, she decided it would be Emily's, for as long as she wanted it to be.

She heard Mr. Ainsworth chuckle as the trio passed through the door out onto the porch. Bradley glanced back over his shoulder once he reached the bottom stair. He gave Claire a faint smile filled with something that looked like love, making her heart take flight on little honeybee wings of hope, but she just could not make herself reach out and catch it.

Bradley was offered a new project from Mr. Parker, who was pleased with his work on Henny House. The builder didn't mind Bradley wasn't able to stay completely true to the home's origins, but he appreciated the effort. "That's why you were hired to handle the projects on existing homes," he told him.

The old county library, housed in Kudzu Creek's original schoolhouse, was moving, and the new owner wanted to restore the building to the way it had looked in 1878 and turn it into a museum. Bradley was the only one at Parker and Associates with the skills to handle this one.

He thumbed through old newspaper articles at his desk until it was time to meet Donovan for their lunch appointment. Bradley had canceled Monday when his lawyer had called about a court date for Emily's guardianship changes. It should have been a celebratory moment, but it was hard to feel happy knowing he would be doing exactly as his mother had warned, raising Emily alone. His father had hinted to him in private that he needed a partner, another mother for his daughter, and that it was past time to start looking. But he didn't have to look. Not for what he wanted.

Claire had been subdued all week. Now that the work was finished on the house, except for the gazebo, he just needed her to make a decision about who would do it and if she still wanted his crew to paint after it was done. She was swamped catching up with the demands for her pottery since most of the inventory had crashed to splinters during the Art Walk, and he understood, but still she hemmed and hawed every time he asked her about finishing up the house. It wouldn't take more than a few days, he reasoned, and though he would likely be in the way, he could swing by to check on things to see Emily and her.

His heart felt like it'd gone through a wood chipper—a mixed debris of happiness, relief and cutting disappointment—and he didn't know how to sort it all out. Something had happened between Claire and him, something so right it was almost magical. Although it was comforting they still had Emily, a link that would bind them forever, he wanted more. Ever since his parents had come, ever since Claire had stood up and declared herself a Henny, things felt different.

She was as polite and kind as ever, but she never lingered to speak with him or called to tell him something Emily had done. They'd gone back to the way things had been when he'd first met her: concentrating on the official business about the little girl with Dori's chin. Claire had thrown up new walls around herself even he couldn't take down.

"Heard about the schoolhouse," Donovan called out as Bradley strolled into Kudzu's with his fists in his pockets. He lifted a hand in greeting, and when he reached the counter, Mac stopped packing a takeout order long enough to push a chocolate milk over.

"You knew I was coming."

"I always know you're on the way if Claire or Donovan are here," she teased.

Bradley pretended to be amused. "I'm that predictable, huh?"

"Being dependable is not a bad thing," Mac told him

as she scurried around the corner. "And where's Claire? I like seeing you two together."

Bradley's heart flinched, but he ignored the hint. Donovan folded his arms and scanned for any possible menu changes on the chalkboard overhead. "Barney's making a fried kudzu and rice dish now."

Bradley wrinkled his nose. "Not for me he's not."

His cousin nudged him. "Try it. It's good with soy sauce."

"No thanks. I may be Southern-fried, but I don't eat kudzu."

"Maybe you should. Did you know it grows a foot a day and the leaves are heart-shaped?"

"So?"

Donovan grinned. "Never mind. You hear from the lawyer?"

Bradley took a breath and made himself smile. "Yes, I meet with a judge in five weeks."

"Great."

Yes, great. Bradley tried to imagine getting Emily to sleep at night in his studio apartment. Claire had agreed to keep Pony. It'd be just him and him alone, with a child that didn't come with blueprints.

As if hearing his thoughts, his cousin asked, "How's Claire? I haven't seen you together much since the Art Walk."

"The house is pretty much done for now, until she has some extra savings put away. She just has to have the gazebo taken down."

"And?"

Bradley shrugged. "I still go over once a day. Usually I eat breakfast or lunch with Emily then play a few minutes until she gets bored or I'm in the way."

"Your parents kind of busted things up, huh?"

Bradley glanced over. "What do you mean? We've worked things out for now."

"I meant with Claire."

"What about Claire?"

Donovan hooted up at the ceiling just as Mac returned and grabbed an order pad. "What'll you have today?" Pen poised, she looked from Donovan to Bradley.

"I'll have fried kudzu and rice," Bradley blurted, his tongue curling. Worst case, he could chase it down with a fruit tart.

Donovan grinned. "I'll have the same." They paid and grabbed their usual seats two tables away from the front window. "So I heard the position on the historical preservation board was filled."

Bradley tried to shake off his pensive attitude. "Yes, they decided to go with someone else."

"Interesting. I wonder if they'll regret it after you restore the old schoolhouse."

Bradley raised a brow at the idea.

His cousin said, "Make them."

"I will," Bradley promised, "because I need something to throw my heart into."

"Because of Claire."

He threw his cousin a disturbed gaze. He hadn't meant to voice his pain out loud. "Things have changed. That's all."

"I can tell you're in love with her."

Hearing it voiced made Bradley's cheeks hot. The depth of his feelings for Claire was something he'd kept close to his heart. He would not go through another failed long-term relationship again because a woman couldn't grow to love him as more than a close friend. When Donovan waited for an answer, Bradley muttered, "Maybe. I guess. But it doesn't matter. The situation is too complicated."

"Complicated how? You're a perfect fit, and you have Emily, too."

"She doesn't feel the same way."

Donovan's eyebrows arched. "I can't believe that. I've watched her with you. You have it bad, and she does, too."

"Evidently not."

"What did she say?" Donovan shifted his gaze to the front window as if he didn't want to make Bradley feel like he was being interrogated.

"Nothing, exactly. Just that Emily and other people are more important, yada yada yada."

Their orders were delivered, and Bradley braced himself to take a bite of the fried rice and greens, hoping the subject was over. The strange taste of fried kudzu made him grimace.

"Well, what did you tell her?" cross-examined Donovan.

"What do you mean?"

"That you love her? Can't live without her? She completes you?" Donovan grinned.

Bradley snorted. "There's no point in telling her how much I do. She'll just..."

Donovan munched his rice. "Let me guess. Change her mind like Dori? Is that what you're afraid of? That you'll have to go down this road by yourself like you did in San Francisco?"

"For someone who shows little interest in settling

down, you sure are interested in my relationships," Bradley retorted.

Swallowing, Donovan laughed. "I still know the real thing when I see it."

"How's that?"

His cousin shrugged. "My parents. Plus, I have a lot of friends who are happily married."

"It's just not worth the risk," Bradley said dismissively.

Kudzu didn't just grow a foot a day; it choked everything else out. They ate in silence a few moments. The food landed like a stone in his stomach.

"You already love her." Donovan was relentless. He took a swig of his soda. "Besides, when have you ever left something unfinished?"

Bradley knew he was right. He couldn't imagine moving forward without Claire in his life. Pretending he was fine with their arrangement was going to make him so miserable that not even being adored by his daughter would stop the pain. Perhaps that was why he'd refused to help with the gazebo for so long. It'd be the end of something wonderful and leave another scar deeper and more tender than the one Dori had left behind.

Bradley realized he didn't care anymore about winning a chair on the board. Whether or not his parents beamed with pride at his accomplishments didn't matter. What mattered most alongside his little girl was the beautiful woman on Maple Grove Lane and what he was going to do about her.

Chapter Twelve

Claire spotted Diane at the crosswalk and waved, surprised to see Vi had also come along for the casual business meeting that would be a walk instead of a lunch date. She'd shied away from seeing them both all week, not wanting to walk past Parker and Associates or run into Bradley at Kudzu's. They already saw each other every morning when he stopped by to spend time with Emily. She took advantage of his visits and left to work in the pottery studio out back, but more because it gave them space than for her workload.

Progress was slow though, and she couldn't blame it on Ms. Olivia's drop-in visits. Claire felt like she'd hit a roadblock, artistically and emotionally. Despite embracing her self-identity and knowing she was a true Henny at Henny House, the work wasn't coming along as she'd hoped because the majority of her heart wasn't in it. How had it happened? How had she fallen in love with Dori's childhood sweetheart? How long would this pain take to fade?

"Hi, Emily!" Vi crouched in front of the stroller after embracing Claire. "Aunt Vi brought you a snack." Emily's eyes widened with excitement. Vi pulled out a granola bar and waved it before her. She glanced up at Claire. "No fruit snacks."

Claire chuckled.

"I have good news," Diane announced. She looked serious about their business walk. Her new tennis shoes were bright pink, and her cropped blue jeans had been replaced with ankle-length yoga pants. Diane motioned in the other direction, away from Alabaster's. "Let's go this way," she suggested. "I want to stop in at the newspaper office and update the image for my business ad."

Claire agreed with relief. She enjoyed walking to the other end of Creek Street.

"Great idea," chimed Vi. "Would you like me to push the stroller?"

"I don't mind at all." Claire smiled. She let go and scurried down the sidewalk between her two friends to keep up with them. Both women were taking this exercise seriously.

"So how is the new line of cruets coming?" huffed Diane. "I've ordered five new flavors of olive oil."

"It's coming along. Not as fast as I'd like it to, but I'm having a hard time coming up with new silhouettes," Claire admitted. "I can't seem to make a decision I feel good about."

"That's interesting," interjected Vi. "Did that start before or after Cici came to visit?" Vi didn't mince words, that was for sure.

"Oh, Vi, Cici came on Art Walk day," Diane chided her. The two women waited for Claire's reply, but she suspected they already knew why.

"It was after," Claire admitted.

"Cici has a way of sticking her nose in things that aren't her business," grumbled Vi.

"Well, she is Emily's grandmother," Claire allowed.

"I don't think that's the only thing she's sticking her nose in," Diane suggested.

Claire pretended she didn't know what she meant. She felt the two women exchange glances across her.

"You know it doesn't matter what your relationship is with Emily when it comes to Bradley," panted Vi after a pause.

"Vi is right," Diane supplied. Her fists were clenched and her elbows bent at the perfect angle to make her pumping arms look square.

Claire felt a stitch in her side. The older women were outpacing her. Another silence fell over them, except for their heavy breathing.

"Claire?" prompted Diane.

"I don't know what you mean."

"Now, Claire. Yes, you do. We mean Bradley. It doesn't matter what his parents think of Dori or yourself. If you love him..."

Vi watched her for a reaction. Claire kept moving forward, one foot after the other, just like she'd done all her life when she'd been pulled out of one home and had to start over in another. "I've just settled down," she said at last.

Emily saved her from having to say more by being a litterbug. The wrapper from the granola bar went sailing by. Vi stopped pushing the stroller and darted back to pick it up off the sidewalk. She crumpled it and shoved it into the stroller's cup holder. "But you do, don't you? Love my nephew?"

The small flickering flame of hope Claire constantly

had to snuff out when Bradley showed up at the door began to glow a little brighter. Emily twisted around in her seat and looked back at her. "Ca-re" she said, as if asking, too.

Claire released a quiet laugh. "Yes, ladies, I do love Bradley. Very much."

"Well, see then!" cheered Diane with delight. "What could be more perfect than falling in love with the father of your child? She is your daughter, you know. Dori gave birth to her, but she is your child now, and who you fall in love with matters a whole lot more than what's happened in the past." She reached over and nudged Vi, and they grinned at each other.

Wanting to escape, Claire started walking again. "It doesn't mean it's reciprocated, not in the same way with the same expectations."

"Are you crazy? Surely you can see how much Bradley adores you." Vi caught up with her, shoving the stroller like it was weightless. "He's home. For good. And he's not the type to walk away from a family or the ones he loves."

Claire knew she was right. Even after escaping to California to sort his life out, he'd returned to Georgia and family and friends. Home.

Diane caught up at last. "Not all families work out, Claire, but surely living here in Kudzu Creek has taught you that most of them do." She grinned. "Bradley Ainsworth is a keeper, if I say so myself."

"He is," Vi promised. "If there's anything about that boy I can tell you, he knows his own mind, and once he's made a choice, it's as good as done. Permanent. *Finito.* Much like you."

Well, I hope he chooses me, Claire almost said, but

she bit it back. She and Bradley had already brought up that possibility, but it'd been put on the back burner, and apparently for good. His parents had made their opinion of her clear, and she knew what happened when a family didn't want you. "Didn't you say you had an announcement, Diane? I received the check from the Art Walk sales, and thank you."

Diane flapped her hand. "I'm just sorry there wasn't more." She motioned toward Emily, who was enjoying the rocket-speed pace. "Thanks to this sweet pea's magic trick with the tablecloth at Art Walk, the majority of it wasn't sellable."

Claire understood. "Yes, next year I vote we not use a tablecloth."

Diane chuckled. "Good idea. Oh, and I do have news for you. Did you know about the Kudzu Creek small business grant they give out every year?"

Claire slanted her head in curiosity. "No, I hadn't thought about looking for grants here, but that's an idea."

"You've been nominated!" Vi interjected.

"Vi!" scolded Diane. "You ruined my surprise!"

"Sorry." Vi wasn't sorry. She laughed over the handle of the stroller. "You see, Claire, you have options here."

Claire stumbled to a stop. They'd reached Kudzu Creek's limits. The cobblestone demarcation line was a thin strip of cement with blacktop continuing on the other side. It was the end of the line. She had to decide to keep going or turn around and go home. To keep plodding along as she had been all her life or to make changes bigger than just moving from one town to another. Heat dampened her shirt. "There's a business grant?"

"Yes," both women crowed at the same time.

"But I don't have a building, I mean, a zoned one. I'm not even an LLC."

"It doesn't matter," Diane explained. "You can register your company later. Every year the Chamber of Commerce gives out a grant to help a new business in town. It can be a home business, a small business or even an artist."

"And get this," interrupted Vi. "It was started by no other than Dr. Henny decades ago!"

"I'm eligible?" Claire wondered in surprise.

"You sure are," said Diane. "Laurel Murphy has really been pushing the art scene the past couple years. It's good for local business and tourism."

"Wow." Hope rippled through Claire. "How much would it be?"

"Enough to cover basic living expenses for one year." Diane stopped, her lips held together with anticipation.

Claire blinked back tears. She could have her own business. She could finish the upstairs of Henny House after all.

"Several of the businesses nominated you," Vi revealed. "Bradley suggested it to Mr. Parker, and he thought so well of you, he spoke with everyone up and down Creek Street."

"Of course, I seconded it," bragged Diane, "and the Fried Kudzu employees made a small donation to the grant in your name."

"Me?" Claire could hardly believe it.

"Why not?" insisted Diane. "You frequent all of our shops, support other small businesses, joined the congregation here in town and, of course, you've given up your personal life to raise a child on your own for another woman."

"You're the perfect candidate," exclaimed Vi.

"Just so you know," announced Diane, "I had a stern word with Laurel after she overlooked Bradley for the board because he didn't have personal ties to anyone on the committee, and we made sure she knew you are just as much a citizen of Kudzu Creek as anyone else."

"Because you are a Henny!" Vi raised a fist in the air.

Claire's eyes watered, and she laughed. "I am!" she agreed. "I am a Henny."

Elated, she pushed away the new and persistent wish that she could be an Ainsworth, too. Really, it was the only thing that kept her from being perfectly happy. But love hurt. She'd lived with that lesson all her life, and losing Dori and Miss Henny had been the exclamation points. She'd just have to deal with her feelings for Bradley until they faded into the background. For Emily's sake. "I couldn't ask for anything more, ladies. Thank you," she told Diane. "Thank you, Vi."

Vi grinned at her. "Call me Aunt Vi, please, and I don't think I can push this stroller another step. It's your turn, Diane. Now let's go to Pruett's and get some blackberry ice cream."

Bradley paced the worn carpet of the library trying to focus on his plans for the renovation project. The building had already closed for the day. Earlier, the sky had looked swollen with rain when he'd hurried inside, and he suspected there was little time before a thundershower exploded overhead.

He studied the false ceiling stained with old leaks. It

looked almost exactly like the kitchen ceiling in Henny House when he'd examined it for damage. Then Claire had walked in, and she would never walk out of his life as long as he had Emily.

The room around him was still, but the air rippled with voices of the past. If he listened hard enough, he could hear them sharing memories and secrets. Bradley let out a quiet breath and padded over to a framed picture of the schoolhouse taken more than a century before. The people in it looked like they belonged to a part of something great. He felt a deep appreciation for the preservation board that had fought to keep the building from being torn down years ago and started a library to make good use of it. He wanted to be a part of something great like that, too; bringing the past into the future and making it beautiful again.

Bradley sighed. But he wanted to be something more than a preservationist and work with his hands. He wanted a family, and without Emily's other half, something would always be missing. He ached inside with a hunger he couldn't name, wondering how long it would take to get over the famished feeling in his body every time he thought of Claire. He had brought his past into the future. He wanted to make it beautiful now. A thump of thunder rattled the library walls. Seconds later, an angry flood of raindrops pounded on the roof. He hoped it held up.

He studied the photograph again and thought about Donovan's remarks. Bradley knew he hadn't been direct with Claire about his feelings, only tried to feel the situation out, and it was out of character for him. That was part of his misery. He'd learned after Dori that every big life decision came with a risk, and his heart had decided after meeting Claire that being rejected by her would have excruciating consequences he didn't want to experience again.

The figures in the schoolhouse photograph grabbed his attention once more. Their pride in Kudzu Creek had preserved a piece of history and made them a part of it. Lake Charles was just a body of water with neighborhoods of stately homes. There was no main street. No old school. No Henny House. No Claire. He wanted her more than anything else—forever.

Lightning struck something nearby outside and Bradley jerked in surprise at the explosion of noise that rattled the windows. The lights flickered then went out. He'd never find another girl like Claire, no matter how long he held his breath, no matter how many houses he tore down and built up again. Like her pottery, Claire Woodbury was an original.

Bradley's legs decided to do something about it before he even finished his train of thought. His heart was in control at last, not his mind filled with so many doubts and fears. He fumbled his way through the darkness past bookcases and a newspaper stand and let himself out the front door. It locked automatically behind him as he stepped onto a small, covered porch.

Rain slammed down from the sky in torrents. The night was black. It looked like Creek Street had lost power. Ducking his head, Bradly jogged for the truck and threw himself inside. He stared at the windshield for a few minutes, his heart pounding as if lightning had struck again. It was time to finish what he'd started on Maple Grove Lane once and for all, or he would never be able to renovate the old schoolhouse the way it should be done. He'd never be able to move on.

* * *

Emily cried out when a bolt of lightning struck outside in the distance. Claire hurried to pick her up out of her high chair. "Hey now, don't worry. It's just Mr. Rainman."

The little girl stuck her thumb in her mouth. "Ca-re," she said, curling her fingers around the collar of Claire's shirt and cradling her head into her neck.

"It's nothing to be afraid of, sweetheart. It's just rain. See?" Claire pointed out the kitchen window, but Emily grunted. "It sounds like it's moving away. Let's go outside and watch."

Claire loved storms. The crackle of electricity in the clouds—as long as it was far away—and the rhythm of the rain were relaxing accompaniments to rocking in a chair on a front porch. She eased open the front door and, hearing the thunder rumble farther off, stepped out. The porch provided the perfect cover. She checked the aluminum rocking chair she'd repainted. It was splattered with stray raindrops.

Emily pointed to the far end of the porch. Bradley had left a pile of fresh lumber to rebuild the corner of the porch after the gazebo was removed. "That," Emily requested, meaning, "Let's go that way."

Claire carried her across the porch to the gazebo. She remembered Bradley had suggested a door from the study on this side of the house and realized it was a good idea. She sighed to herself. She really didn't want to have the gazebo torn down, she admitted. It was a part of Miss Henny's precious memories, and lately, Claire had been creating her own memories beneath its tapered rooftop.

Emily squirmed to get down once they reached

the gazebo, and Claire set her free. Curtains of water poured over the sides of the gingerbread trim. Emily began to sing and skip in circles. Claire joined her. They twirled around to the music of the rain until the deluge thinned and finally trickled out. Claire was breathless. She laughed and stumbled—right into someone's arms.

"Daddy!"

Surprised, Claire looked up into Bradley's face. He didn't seem to hear Emily. She felt his long, slim fingers on her elbows. In the dim light of a lamp in the study's window, she saw his dark gaze locked onto hers, ripe with emotion.

Emily clapped her hands, shouted, "Go," and loped across the porch toward the other end. Her usual routine was to frolic back and forth in front of the front door, stopping intermittently to push the doorbell. Maybe she hadn't noticed her father and Claire were frozen like statues in one another's grip.

Bradley bit his top lip, to dry it maybe, or perhaps he was nervous. His damp shirt suggested he'd been out in the rain. "You're wet," Claire observed.

"It's raining."

"It is. I mean it was earlier," Claire stammered, unnerved by how close he held her. Around them, the crickets picked up where the raindrops left off. She fingered his damp sleeves and tried to step away, but she couldn't. Why had Vi and Diane given her hope?

"We need to talk," Bradley said in a determined tone.

"Okay." Claire's stomach sank. Emily was still enjoying her romp on the porch. "Here in the gazebo?"

"If you like, and I want you to know I don't care about the gazebo anymore. I'll tear it down myself, paint it purple, whatever you want. That's why I came.

I want you to know I'd do anything for you. Your happiness matters more to me than saving a pile of wood."

Claire felt her mouth twitch, but he didn't smile. He was serious. He would tear down something he held sacred just to please her? "You didn't get on the historical preservation board. Vi told me about it."

"No."

"I'm sorry, Bradley."

"That's not why I'm here."

Claire took a shallow breath. "Why are you here? Are you going to tear this thing down now?"

"No. I needed to tell you why I managed this project even though you only kept some of the floors original."

"To see Emily," Claire assumed.

"Not just her."

Claire's heart quivered, and her stomach tied itself into a tight knot to avoid getting stung. She must not hope too hard. She remembered Mrs. Ainsworth's declaration. *So you have no family.* If the woman was right, she would only ever have the house and a little piece of Emily.

"I loved Emily before I even knew she was mine..." Bradley began, "the moment I saw her standing beside you, gazing up at me with Dori's smile." He slid his fingers down Claire's arms and encircled her wrists. "I fell for you the moment you tumbled off the porch of this old house and into my arms." He chuckled low in his throat and stole a glance over his shoulder toward Emily, who was marching back and forth behind them.

Claire's breath caught in her throat when he dipped his chin lower to her face.

"Then we happened."

Her heart sang. It didn't even wait for the next line,

the exception, the *but*... He looked intently into her eyes and Claire's knees began to rattle. Could a man like Bradley really want a girl like her forever?

"Claire, I love you. I need help raising Emily, I do, and I promise never to take her out of your life. But I know you and I could have something more wonderful and everlasting than just sharing the life of our little girl, more sturdy and dependable than this beautiful house and your Miss Henny."

Claire thought she would faint. Her mind and heart cried *yes* as one. Her eyes teared against her will. She simply could not speak, but she could feel her pulse throbbing all the way to the ends of her fingertips.

"I could do that, Claire, easily. I love you," Bradley repeated huskily. He moved close enough to touch the tip of her nose with his. "The way you put others before yourself. The way you stand by your convictions. Your kindness and, my gosh, your strength and fortitude. Not everyone could have survived a childhood like yours without becoming defensive or bitter. Not everyone would give up their entire life and take in a child to raise on their own."

His voice became ragged with raw emotion, and his eyes watered over with frustration. It wrung out her heart. "You have given me everything by loving Emily, and I'm asking you to give me a chance and trust that you can love me, too."

Claire forced back a small, eager sob that almost escaped her throat.

Bradley shook his head as if running out of the words he needed to convince her. "I can't see my life without you in it. It would never make sense, never be complete. So I'm asking you, telling you, that you are not just a most trusted friend, but my dream girl, the woman of my dreams that I never knew I could have. I have feelings for you that are just so..." A single tear escaped and traveled down his cheek. "I love you, Claire, and I'm asking you if you love me, too. If you will give me a chance to show you that I can be your family and..." He hesitated, as if just now seeing he'd hypnotized her, and lowered his mouth to hers. "So much more," he finished in a whisper.

Claire did not fight it. She didn't think or worry or try to sort it out. She let her eyes close and leaned into him, accepting everything he had to offer in one single kiss of promise and commitment. Henny House was hers. Emily was hers. And at last, the man she had completely lost her heart to was hers and hers alone.

"I love you," she murmured.

"Forever?" he pleaded.

"Forever and a day," she promised.

She forced her eyes open, surprised to find herself in the same dream she'd lost herself in. "I love you, Bradley Ainsworth, as much as I love your daughter and more."

He wrapped his arms around her. The rain returned as if it'd held back only long enough for them to come together. Emily approached, out of breath and whimpering. She threw her arms around their legs, and Bradley paused to pick her up with a low chuckle. The three of them danced slowly around until the little girl began to yawn, and it was past time for her to go to bed.

"Bradley," Claire whispered later after Emily had fallen asleep, "I think I'm going to keep the gazebo."

"That's wonderful news." Bradley sounded indifferent. He rubbed his palm up and down her back while they rested on the parlor sofa watching lightning color the sky through the window. "And how about another door?" He took her hand and kissed it.

"Yes," Claire answered in a soft tone saturated with happiness, "in the study." She swallowed and added in a hesitant whisper, "Your study, if you want it."

"Mine?" Bradley wondered in a teasing voice that sounded pleased. "I've always wanted to be a part of Henny House. Now more than ever."

Claire's heart pattered against his. What more could she say to show him how much she wanted him?

"I have one condition, though," Bradley informed her. "It would be even more perfect if I could be a Henny, and you became an Ainsworth."

Claire felt her lips stretch into a tender smile and her heart burned. "It's what I've always wanted."

Bradley lowered his face to hers and brushed a thumb across her cheekbone. "Then marry me, Claire Henny, and become the mother of *all* my children."

Her eyes flooded with tears with no room left to hold her happiness. "I will," she promised, "and no one will ever take down that gazebo as long as I live."

Bradley laughed deep in the back of his throat and dropped a tender kiss on her lips. "Won't Kudzu Creek be happy?"

Claire curled a smile into a mischievous grin. "I didn't say I wouldn't paint it purple though."

Epilogue

Autumn swept into Kudzu Creek late as usual, turning the crowns of the treetops on Maple Grove Lane scarlet just in time to accent the purple and teal bows tied to the front porch of Henny House. The eggplant-painted door swung open, and Ms. Olivia stopped her pacing and patted her hairpiece down. She smiled at Vi with approval. Vi beamed at the little girl at her side before leading her over the threshold. Ms. Olivia took Emily's other hand, and the trio marched solemnly down the length of the porch to the grand gazebo where Diane waited with a basket of petals for the little flower girl.

Bradley blinked back tears and tried to contain the lump growing in his throat. Emily looked up fondly at him when she reached his polished loafers and offered a handful of flowers. "Here, Daddy." He smiled and reached for them, squeezing her little hand.

A small gasp from those standing around him made his heart skip a beat, and Bradley straightened, glancing at his best man for support. Donovan gave him an encouraging nod. The heads of those seated along the porch turned, and Bradley followed their gazes. His damp palms trembled.

Like a vision, Claire stood solemnly by the bronze plaque engraved with the name of their home beside the door. Beneath *Henny House*, the second line, *Artist in Residence,* gleamed in the afternoon sunlight. The sunbeams made her fair hair glimmer. Now down to her jawline, she'd pulled a single lock of it back with a glittery hairpin that sparkled like a diamond.

His tight throat became unbearable, and Bradley's eyes filled with tears. Beside his bride-to-be, Mr. Thu gave a slight bow, smiled widely at everyone then took Claire by the elbow. The pair walked in time to a violin sonata echoing from the speakers his father had helped set up the day before.

Bradley watched his future walk straight into his arms. He nearly cried when Claire took his hand. Aunt Vi's tears were already streaming. His mother sat in the first row, straight and beaming with pride.

It seemed all of Kudzu Creek surrounded him with his parents and cousins. He had eyes for no one but Claire, but he was aware of everyone around them and knew Miss Henny and Dori were watching from their framed photographs along the porch railing.

Diane and her husband stood a few feet back should Vi need help with Emily. Mr. Thu took a seat beside Ms. Olivia who leaned over and said something about the wedding dress she'd approved in an audible whisper. From the back, Mac and Barney had left the kitchen long enough to listen to the vows.

Claire squeezed his hand, and Bradley realized he'd been so mesmerized by her face, he hadn't taken in the rest of the details. The crisp white wedding gown was long, fitted in all the right places and flared at the ankles. A scooped neck accented a round glass-bubble necklace she'd fired in her own kiln. Soft and dreamlike, long sheer sleeves made her arms look slender all the way to where they touched her wrists.

"You look beautiful," he murmured. He squeezed her fingers back and studied her trembling hands. The engagement ring he'd purchased for her was antique with a stone of her favorite color, a perfectly preserved amethyst framed by tiny diamonds.

"Thank you," she said in a breathless voice. Her cheeks were flushed and shining like apples, her blue-green eyes sparkling with emotion. "So do you," she said in a serious tone. He chuckled to hold back a small sob of emotion.

"Me, too," insisted a sweet voice at their feet.

Bradley realized Emily was watching his greatest wish unfold. He prayed he could make all her dreams come true. Before the pastor began, he bent and picked up his little girl. He had promises to make, but they weren't just to the woman he wanted, the woman who had kept her promise to his and Dori's child. They were to the daughter he loved with all his heart and his forever family.

* * * * *

Dear Reader,

The creeping vines of kudzu are a staple ingredient of the Southern landscape. The leaves and flowers really are edible, but let's leave those to the goats and stick with dandelion tea, thank you. This story came to me after crossing a bridge called Kudzu Creek on a weekend road trip. If there's anything more charming than a rural Main Street, it's a catchy name, and around here, we have them by the bushel. Creating Bradley and Claire came easily, too. We all love to see the prodigal son come home, and every girl deserves love, devotion, and her sphere of maternal influence no matter what role she's destined to play. I love Bradley's good heart and passionate ambitions. Claire reminds me of everything I treasure about being a mother and homemaker.

This story was inspired by my own mother, who experienced the foster care system of the 1950s and sacrificed everything to have a family. Thanks, Mom. Heartfelt gratitude also goes to my husband, who supports my wandering and writing; my kids, for tolerating my hobbies and distractions, and friends who buy my books and say kind things. Last but not least, thank you to the editors at Love Inspired for pushing me, challenging me, and giving me the opportunity to publish my stories.

If I'm a new-to-you author, I hope you enjoyed my second release with Love Inspired. Let's connect. I love chatting with readers on Facebook (https://www.facebook.

com/danielle.thorne.184) or through my website at www.daniellethorne.com, so look me up.

Warmly,
Danielle Thorne

COMING NEXT MONTH FROM **Love Inspired**

THE AMISH MATCHMAKER'S CHOICE

Redemption's Amish Legacies • by Patricia Johns

Newly returned to the Amish community, Jake Knussli must find a wife in six months or lose his uncle's farm. Can matchmaker Adel Draschel secure a *frau* for him—before losing her own heart to the handsome farmer?

THEIR PRETEND COURTSHIP

The Amish of New Hope • by Carrie Lighte

Pressured by her stepfather to court, Eliza Keim begrudgingly walks out with blueberry farmer Jonas Kanagy—except Jonas is only trying to protect his brother from what he thinks are Eliza's heartbreaker ways. When the two are forced to make their courtship in name only look real, they may discover more than they bargained for...

GUARDING HIS SECRET

K-9 Companions • by Jill Kemerer

When Wyoming rancher Randy Watkins finds himself caring for his surprise baby nephew, he seeks the help of longtime friend Hannah Carr. But when her retired service dog seems to sense all is not right with Randy's health, will he trust Hannah with the truth?

THE RANCHER'S FAMILY LEGACY

The Ranchers of Gabriel Bend • by Myra Johnson

Building contractor Mark Caldwell is ready to inherit his grandfather's horse ranch and put his traumatic past behind him—if he can survive working in Texas Hill Country for a year. But when his dog bonds with local caterer Holly Elliot's son, can they put aside their differences and open their hearts?

HER MOUNTAIN REFUGE

by Laurel Blount

Widowed, pregnant and under the thumb of her controlling mother-in-law, Charlotte Tremaine needs help—but she doesn't expect it to come from her estranged childhood best friend. Yet letting Sheriff Logan Carter whisk her away to his foster mother's remote mountain home might be her best chance at a fresh start...

A MOTHER FOR HIS SON

by Betty Woods

In town to help her grandmother, chef Rachel Landry plans to use the time to heal her broken heart—not help Mac Greer with his guest ranch. But her growing affection for his little boy could be just the push she needs to once again see the possibility of something more...

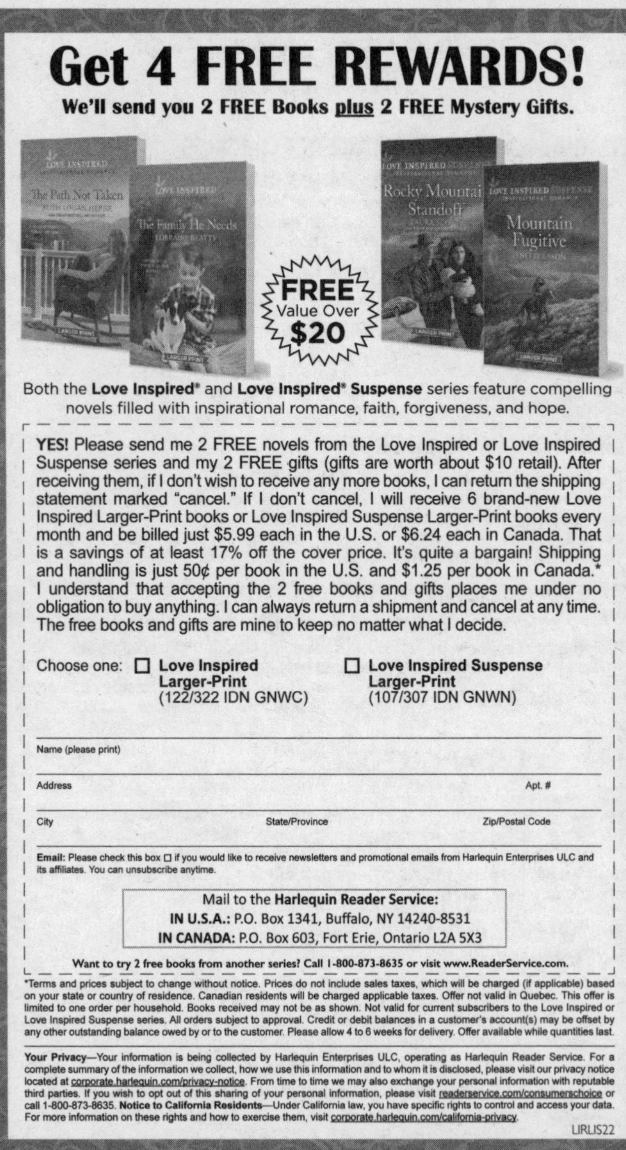
Get 4 FREE REWARDS!
We'll send you 2 FREE Books plus 2 FREE Mystery Gifts.
LOVE INSPIRED
The Path Not Taken
LOVE INSPIRED
The Family He Needs
LOVE INSPIRED SUSPENSE
Standoff
LOVE INSPIRED SUSPENSE
Mountain Fugitive
FREE
Value Over
$20
Both the Love Inspired® and Love Inspired® Suspense series feature compelling novels filled with inspirational romance, faith, forgiveness, and hope.
YES! Please send me 2 FREE novels from the Love Inspired or Love Inspired Suspense series and my 2 FREE gifts (gifts are worth about $10 retail). After receiving them, if I don't wish to receive any more books, I can return the shipping statement marked "cancel." If I don't cancel, I will receive 6 brand-new Love Inspired Larger-Print books or Love Inspired Suspense Larger-Print books every month and be billed just $5.99 each in the U.S. or $6.24 each in Canada. That is a savings of at least 17% off the cover price. It's quite a bargain! Shipping and handling is just 50¢ per book in the U.S. and $1.25 per book in Canada.* I understand that accepting the 2 free books and gifts places me under no obligation to buy anything. I can always return a shipment and cancel at any time. The free books and gifts are mine to keep no matter what I decide.
Choose one: ☐ Love Inspired Larger-Print (122/322 IDN GNWC)
☐ Love Inspired Suspense Larger-Print (107/307 IDN GNWN)
Name (please print)
Address
Apt. #
City
State/Province
Zip/Postal Code
Email: Please check this box ☐ if you would like to receive newsletters and promotional emails from Harlequin Enterprises ULC and its affiliates. You can unsubscribe anytime.
Mail to the Harlequin Reader Service:
IN U.S.A.: P.O. Box 1341, Buffalo, NY 14240-8531
IN CANADA: P.O. Box 603, Fort Erie, Ontario L2A 5X3
Want to try 2 free books from another series? Call 1-800-873-8635 or visit www.ReaderService.com.
*Terms and prices subject to change without notice. Prices do not include sales taxes, which will be charged (if applicable) based on your state or country of residence. Canadian residents will be charged applicable taxes. Offer not valid in Quebec. This offer is limited to one order per household. Books received may not be as shown. Not valid for current subscribers to the Love Inspired or Love Inspired Suspense series. All orders subject to approval. Credit or debit balances in a customer's account(s) may be offset by any other outstanding balance owed by or to the customer. Please allow 4 to 6 weeks for delivery. Offer available while quantities last.
Your Privacy—Your information is being collected by Harlequin Enterprises ULC, operating as Harlequin Reader Service. For a complete summary of the information we collect, how we use this information and to whom it is disclosed, please visit our privacy notice located at corporate.harlequin.com/privacy-notice. From time to time we may also exchange your personal information with reputable third parties. If you wish to opt out of this sharing of your personal information, please visit readerservice.com/consumerschoice or call 1-800-873-8635. Notice to California Residents—Under California law, you have specific rights to control and access your data. For more information on these rights and how to exercise them, visit corporate.harlequin.com/california-privacy.
LIRLIS22

When Wyoming rancher Randy Watkins finds himself in a bind, he seeks the help of longtime friend Hannah Carr. But when her retired service dog seems to sense all is not right with his health, will he trust Hannah with the truth?

Read on for a sneak peek at the next K-9 Companions book, Guarding His Secret, *by Jill Kemerer!*

"What do I need to know?" Hannah faced him then, her big blue eyes full of expectation. Randy liked that about her. She didn't hide anything.

Well, everyone hid something. He'd certainly been hiding something for years—from this town, from his friends, even from his brother.

So what? It was nobody's business.

"Let's start with the basics." He gave her a quick tour. Her presence was making his pulse race. He didn't like it or the reason why it was happening.

Hannah's cell phone rang. "Do you mind if I take this?"

"Go ahead." He backed up to give her privacy, busying himself with a box of nets, but he could hear every word she said.

"You're kidding," she said breathlessly. "That's great news. Yes…Right now? I'd love to…You're serious? I can't believe it…"

Finally, she ended the conversation and turned to him with shining eyes. "That was Molly. She has a dog for me."

"Another puppy?" He placed the box on the counter.

"No, a retired service dog." She looked ready to float through the air. "I've been on the adoption list forever. The ones that have become available all went to either their original puppy raiser or someone higher on the list."

"Won't the dog be old?" Why would she want someone's ancient dog that might not live long?

"Some of them are. This one is eight. Too old to be placed for service, but he's still got a lot of good years left."

Something told him that even if the dog had only a couple of good months left, Hannah would be equally enthusiastic.

"I'm going to go pick him up." She lightly clapped her hands in happiness, and he kind of wished he could go with her.

"Let me get you the store key, then."

"Oh, wait." She winced. "I didn't think this through. Is there any way I can bring him with me to the store? He passed all of his obedience classes years ago. I'm sure he wouldn't cause any trouble. I just can't imagine bringing him home and then leaving him by himself all day before he has a chance to get to know me. He's used to being with someone all the time."

"Of course. Bring him." He'd always liked dogs. His customers wouldn't mind. In fact, they'd probably linger in the store even more because of him. Maybe he'd get a dog of his own after he moved into the new house. It was a thought.

"Thanks." She came over and gave him a quick hug. "I'll open the store tomorrow at nine. You're closed on Sundays, right?"

"Right." He stood frozen from the shock of her touch as she hurried to the back. The sound of the screen door slamming jolted him out of his stupor.

Hannah almost made him forget he wasn't like any other guy.

And he wasn't.

He had a secret. And that secret would stay with him until the day he died.

When that day came, he'd be single.

He had to be more careful around Hannah Carr. There was something about her that made his logic disappear like the morning dew. He couldn't afford to forget he couldn't have her.